"What about me?" Naomi — "...— off of me, you son of a bitch?"

Longarm looked at Burt and smiled. "I love it when she talks dirty."

"I don't have the handcuff key," Burt reminded him.

Longarm nodded and dug the key out of his vest pocket. He handed it over to Burt, who unfastened the handcuffs and ushered the girl into her room. Burt closed the door and set his chair in front of it. "I'll be fine down here. Go on now. Get some sleep."

Six hours later Longarm woke up, quickly washed and dressed, and went back downstairs to the hotel kitchen. The chair in front of Naomi's room was empty.

Inside the room he found Burt lying on the floor, his trousers around his ankles.

And no sign of Naomi Foster . . .

DON'T MISS THESE
ALL-ACTION WESTERN SERIES
FROM THE BERKLEY PUBLISHING GROUP

THE GUNSMITH by J. R. Roberts
Clint Adams was a legend among lawmen, outlaws, and ladies. They called him . . . the Gunsmith.

LONGARM by Tabor Evans
The popular long-running series about Deputy U.S. Marshal Custis Long—his life, his loves, his fight for justice.

SLOCUM by Jake Logan
Today's longest-running action Western. John Slocum rides a deadly trail of hot blood and cold steel.

BUSHWHACKERS by B. J. Lanagan
An action-packed series by the creators of Longarm! The rousing adventures of the most brutal gang of cutthroats ever assembled—Quantrill's Raiders.

DIAMONDBACK by Guy Brewer
Dex Yancey is Diamondback, a Southern gentleman turned con man when his brother cheats him out of the family fortune. Ladies love him. Gamblers hate him. But nobody pulls one over on Dex . . .

WILDGUN by Jack Hanson
The blazing adventures of mountain man Will Barlow—from the creators of Longarm!

TEXAS TRACKER by Tom Calhoun
J.T. Law: the most relentless—and dangerous—manhunter in all Texas. Where sheriffs and posses fail, he's the best man to bring in the most vicious outlaws—for a price.

TABOR EVANS

LONGARM

AND THE
LADY LAWBREAKER

JOVE BOOKS, NEW YORK

THE BERKLEY PUBLISHING GROUP
Published by the Penguin Group
Penguin Group (USA) LLC
375 Hudson Street, New York, New York 10014

USA • Canada • UK • Ireland • Australia • New Zealand • India • South Africa • China

penguin.com

A Penguin Random House Company

LONGARM AND THE LADY LAWBREAKER

A Jove Book / published by arrangement with the author

For information, address: The Berkley Publishing Group,
a division of Penguin Group (USA) LLC,
375 Hudson Street, New York, New York 10014.

ISBN: 978-0-515-15483-2

PUBLISHING HISTORY
Jove mass-market edition / August 2014

PRINTED IN THE UNITED STATES OF AMERICA

10 9 8 7 6 5 4 3 2 1

Cover illustration by Milo Sinovcic.

Chapter 1

Custis Long yawned. Stretched. His eyelids fluttered as he fought against sleep. He had to get up soon and head for his own bed. In the meantime he was sated. Maria Lourdes Consuela Valdes lay tucked in close beside him, her breathing slow and steady in the aftermath of their coupling.

Chill night air cooled the thin film of sweat on his flesh and somewhere on the street below he heard the sounds of a horse's passage. Life could not get much better than this, he thought.

The deputy United States marshal known as Longarm yawned again and rolled his head to the side. Maria Lourdes's nipple jutted high off her left tit. The woman had the longest nipples he had ever seen. Sensitive, too. He considered toying with this one, but if he did that, he was likely to wake the lady. And Longarm was just too worn-out already to want another piece of that. Maria Lourdes was wild, but she could suck the life out of a man. She certainly had drained Longarm.

Forcing himself to move, he swiveled onto the side of the

feather bed and sat upright. Yawned again and scratched. Then he reached down and silently gathered up his clothes and his boots.

He padded barefoot out of Maria Lourdes's sleeping chamber to the outer room of her suite and stopped there to dress. He perched on the edge of a flimsy-looking chair to pull on his boots, stood again, and barely remembered in time to stop himself from stamping his feet firmly into the boots lest the noise disturb Maria Lourdes.

Longarm stretched again and decided maybe he was waking up after all. For a minute or so there it had seemed in doubt.

There was not enough light in the room to check himself in the mirror as only a very low flame burned in a single lamp, so he had to straighten his collar and tie by feel. And long habit made him check the position of the .45-caliber Colt that rode at his waist, his fingertips finding the polished walnut grips exactly where they should be, just left of his belt buckle with his holster canted for a cross draw.

Once that was done he declared himself ready to face the world.

Custis Long stood well over six feet in height, lean and whipcord tough with broad shoulders and narrow hips. His features were craggy, tanned by years of exposure to the elements. He had brown hair and a brown handlebar mustache. His eyes could seem golden brown at times . . . or cold steel at others.

He wore brown corduroy trousers, a brown tweed coat and checkerboard shirt. His gun belt was black leather, as were his knee-high cavalry boots. On his head he wore a flat-crowned brown Stetson.

Once into the upstairs hallway in Maria Lourdes's rented house—she was in Denver for a month or two to shop, she said—he paused to extract a long, slender cheroot from his inside coat pocket. He bit the twist off the tip and deposited the speck of tobacco into a decorative urn on the landing, struck a lucifer, and lighted his smoke, grateful for the flavor of it after being without for some hours. Maria Lourdes, it seemed, did not care for the scent of tobacco.

On the ground floor he smiled and nodded to one of the lady's housemaids, this one small and dark and wearing a frilly apron over a plain black dress. She had flour up to her wrists and he supposed she was busy setting dough for Maria Lourdes's morning biscuits.

It must be grand, he thought, to be rich and have a staff of house help to do every little thing for you. It was something he would never know. And really did not care.

Maria Lourdes's wealth and below-the-border genteel upbringing did not, however, keep her from liking to fuck like a crazed mink. After a very casual meeting in a café close to the state capitol building, she had worn Longarm near to a frazzle.

Not that he minded.

Now, however, he wanted to go home. Go to bed. And get a deep, if not a long, sleep before he reported in to the office in the morning. He had been idle here in Denver for several weeks now and was looking forward to an assignment.

He smiled a little, remembering the evening. And the lady. Then he let himself out into the night.

Chapter 2

Longarm woke too late to have breakfast at his boarding-house. By the time he went downstairs the dining room table had already been cleared and he could hear the sounds of clattering dishes from the kitchen. Not that he wanted anything to eat. His stomach was still bilious after the previous evening's indulgences, and his mouth tasted like someone had shit in it.

Rather than going out to the street he went out the back way and around to the side of the back porch to where wash-water was dumped. A patch of mint grew in the shade there. He bent and plucked a few stems. Chewing them sweetened his mouth considerably.

From there he walked around to the front of the house and waved to a hansom driver who was sitting in the driving box of his rig half a block distant.

"Federal Building," he ordered as he climbed into the cab.

"Coming right up, gov'nor," the driver said. As soon as Longarm closed the cab door the driver snapped his whip above the ears of his horse, and the vehicle lurched into motion, swaying on its leather springs like a ship in a storm.

It was only a short drive to the imposing, gray-stone U.S. Federal Building on Colfax Avenue.

Longarm paid the cabbie and tried to rub the sleep out of his eyes before he mounted the broad steps and entered the building.

The United States marshals' office was on the first floor. Longarm pulled the door open and stepped inside.

"Mornin', Henry," he said to the office manager, hanging his Stetson on the hat rack near the door.

"Barely," the bespectacled clerk responded.

"What?"

"Barely morning," Henry said. "You're late."

"Not very," Longarm said.

"Late enough to annoy the boss. He's been asking for you."

Longarm immediately brightened and asked hopefully, "He has an assignment for me?"

"That's not for me to say, but I'll tell him you're here."

Longarm snorted. Not for Henry to say, perhaps, but he most certainly knew. Henry knew everything that went on in U.S. Marshal Billy Vail's office. Everything. Maybe everything that went on in the whole building, too, or so it sometimes seemed.

Henry rose from behind his desk, lightly tapped on the door leading back to Billy's office, paused there for only a moment before he disappeared inside leaving Longarm alone in the outer office. When he emerged again he stopped to gather some papers from his desk before once again entering Billy's private domain. Finally he returned and motioned for Longarm to enter.

"'Bout time," Longarm mumbled as he went in to see the former Texas Ranger who was his boss.

Chapter 3

Billy Vail—United States Marshal William Vail—sat behind his desk, bald and almost cherubic in appearance. He looked as though he would be squeamish about stepping on a bug, much less sending a .45 slug into the belly of a man. In fact Vail had more than held his own in the rough-and-ready world of the Texas Rangers before securing this appointment as marshal.

To his great disgust, once in the job Billy found that the demands of the office kept him mostly behind a desk acting more as an administrator than a hunter of men. He did the job well, though, and his deputies would have followed Vail into the gates of hell itself. Moreover, they knew that if such a thing were ever to become necessary, Billy Vail would be out in front leading the way.

"Mornin', Boss." Longarm fought down an impulse to salute.

Vail looked up from the papers on his desk and grunted. Loudly. Longarm was not entirely sure how he should interpret that so he kept his mouth shut and waited for Billy to speak.

Vail took his time about addressing his deputy, who was generally regarded as delivering the best results among the many deputies assigned to the Denver District . . . even if not always by approved methods.

Finally Billy leaned back, the springs beneath his swivel chair creaking in protest, and laced his fingers behind his head. "You've been sitting around with your thumb up your backside for more than long enough, Custis, so it is about time you get out into the field again."

"Yes, sir, I agree," Longarm said.

"I have something for you."

"Yes, sir, thank you, sir."

Billy grunted again. Swiveled his chair around to face out of the window for a moment, then again swung around to face Longarm. "This is not something I would normally give to you, Custis. You tend to go your own way with things and never mind the book. Or plain common sense."

"Yes, sir."

"So this time I want you to make an exception. This time I want you to do things exactly the way you are supposed to. No ad libbing, please."

"Boss, I don't have any idea what you're talkin' about."

"Do you know something, Custis. Sad as I am to say it, I believe you. You really don't have any grasp of proper law enforcement procedure." Billy shook his head, took a deep breath and went on. "We have a new deputy assigned to this office. He needs to be . . . I was about to say he should be broken in, but I'm afraid if I do that you will take me at my word and end up really breaking him."

"Oh, now really. Boss. I—"

"Quiet, please."

"Yes, sir."

"What I am asking you to do is simple enough, Custis. I

want you to take the young man out with you. The assignment the two of you will complete is simplicity itself. You will pick up a prisoner and transport her back here for trial."

"Yes, sir."

"And you will do it without trauma or drama or anything else. Just nice and easy and give the young man a taste of the life."

"As you say, sir." Longarm had learned long ago that a liberal sprinkling of "sirs" into any conversation tended to keep things calm and took nothing away from the speaker. "I don't think I've met this, um, new deputy, sir."

"None of us has," Billy said. "The reason for that is . . . complicated."

"How is that, sir?"

"Our new deputy is the nephew of a gentleman in Wyoming who is a major player in that territory's push to become a state. He . . . the uncle, that is . . . is the one who secured the young man's appointment."

"And the kid?" Longarm asked. "Does he want t' enforce the law? Or just t' wear a badge on his chest an' strut around for all the girls t' see?"

Billy shrugged. "I expect you will find out before I do."

"Come again, sir?"

"You will be the first to actually meet him. In Cheyenne. You are to go there and, um, pick him up. He will be registered at the Graythorne Inn. You will meet him there and take him with you on a field assignment."

Longarm raised an eyebrow.

"It is a simple enough thing. You . . . and C. Burton Hood . . . are to proceed to Thermopolis and pick up a prisoner the town marshal is holding for us. Then you will bring the prisoner back here for trial."

"And this prisoner?" Longarm asked.

"Her name is Naomi Foster. She is accused of stealing from the mail when she was employed as a postal clerk in Buffalo."

"Buffalo, New York, sir?"

"Buffalo, Wyoming Territory," Vail corrected.

"Ah! One o' my favorite towns," Longarm said. "Anything special about this new deputy that I should know?" he asked.

"If I knew more I would tell you, Custis."

"He's already taken the oath?" Longarm asked.

"No, not yet."

"But you want him t' go out with me anyway," Longarm said slowly, chewing on his thoughts as he spoke.

Billy nodded. "I do."

"An' you want me t' handle things strictly by the book this time."

"That's right."

Longarm sighed. "The Graythorne Inn in Cheyenne. C. Burton Hood."

"Exactly." Billy leaned back in his chair. Longarm was not entirely positive, but he thought the boss had a look about him, something on the order of a cat with a fluff of canary feathers around its mouth. There was something—Longarm did not know what—that Billy was not telling him. But that he was expected to figure out on his own.

"An' this Thermopolis place, Boss. Where the hell is it?"

"It is approximately at the end of the earth. Somewhere between the Big Horns and the Wind River Reservation," Vail said. "Luckily for you, there is a stagecoach that runs there. You can take the train west to Rawlins and a stagecoach north from there."

"Yes, sir."

"And, um, good luck, Custis."

"Thank you, Boss. Not that I expect t' need luck on a simple assignment like this," Longarm said.

"I hope you are right about that, Custis. Now see Henry on your way out. He has your travel papers in hand."

Again Longarm had to resist that impulse to salute as he turned and headed out of the office.

Chapter 4

Longarm had plenty of time to think on his way to Cheyenne. He concluded that Billy's plan was not a matter of
being devious—although the boss was certainly capable of
that if or when need be—but of good management.

The prisoner being a woman, standard operating procedure was that whenever possible two deputies be assigned
to transport her. That was to avoid any claims later by some
lying bitch that she had been molested while she was in
custody. Longarm had seen that sort of thing happen more
than once. One of those times the lie nearly ruined the career
of a good man.

By sending this untried youngster C. Burton Hood on
the detail, Billy could comply with that procedure without
wasting the services of two good deputies. Instead he sent
his top deputy and the kid. The prisoner need never know
that Hood was not a sworn officer.

That had to be in Billy's mind when he handed out the
assignment, Longarm concluded.

Still, Billy had looked . . . well, damnit, he had looked

devious back there in Denver. Was there something about this deal that Longarm did not yet understand? Could be, he conceded with a sigh. Whatever came, though, would have to play out however it chose. All Longarm could do was his duty.

That much decided, he got up and walked back to the smoking car where he found a steward who was serving a decent brand of whiskey and a table of gentlemen playing a friendly game of low-stakes poker.

"Got room for another?" Longarm asked, drink in one hand and cheroot in the other.

"Welcome, friend. Sit down and join us."

Longarm stuck his cigar between his teeth at a jaunty angle and grinned as he sat.

Chapter 5

"I am sorry, sir. Mr. Hood is out."

"Any idea when he'll be back?"

"No, sir, none."

Longarm grunted his disappointment, then said, "All right. Reckon I'll wait." He picked up his carpetbag and headed for the bank of easy chairs arranged in the Graythorne Inn's lobby.

"Sir," the desk clerk called to him.

Longarm stopped. Turned. "Yes?"

"I don't know when Mr. Hood will return, but . . . it could be morning. Or later."

"I see. All right, thanks." Longarm changed direction back out toward the street. It was obvious from the look of the place that the Graythorne was more expensive than Henry would allow on his expense account when he returned to Denver. He needed to find something he—and the government—could afford.

Past experience led him back toward Front Street and the Pickering Hotel. As soon as he walked through the doors there the desk clerk smiled and said, "Marshal Long, welcome. It is good to see you again, sir."

"It's good t' see you, too, Jimmy."

Jimmy tapped the bell that sat on his desk and a moment later a chubby bellboy emerged from the hotel office. "Take Marshal Long's bag up to number four, Eric." To Longarm he said, "Do you want to go up now, Marshal, or would you like to have supper first?"

"I'll go upstairs an' have a wash now, but I'm lookin' forward to one o' your fine meals after rattling around on a train all afternoon."

"Very good. Eric, take a pitcher of water for the marshal, too." And again to Longarm, "Would you like a bath before supper?"

"No, I'll just wash off in the basin some."

Jimmy managed to give the impression that this was the most sensible thing he had heard all day. But then Jimmy Smith was an exceptional hotel manager. He made people want to return to the Pickering. Longarm suspected that he owned the place or at least a piece of it.

"Thanks, Jimmy." Longarm followed the bellboy up to his room and tipped the kid a nickel, then quickly washed the soot of rail travel off his face and neck and went back downstairs for supper.

He thought about trying to locate Hood at the Graythorne again but decided against it. The new deputy would wait for morning. So would their prisoner, already in custody in Thermopolis.

Which left Longarm on his own for an evening in Cheyenne.

He was smiling as he went outside and strode purposefully up the street.

Chapter 6

His knock was answered by a small woman with dark eyes and dusky skin. She wore a frilly apron and had a cloth wrapped turban-like around her head.

"Yes, sir. May I tell the missus who is calling, please?"

Longarm gave his name and waited outside for the maid's return. Instead of the maid, however, he was greeted by a smiling matron with hair that was beginning to gray at the temples. She was wearing a dress of dark blue silk. She held her hands out to take both of his.

"Custis, dear, how long has it been?" She laughed. "I'll tell you how long. *Too* long, that is how long it has been. Come in, please."

"I agree," he told her. "It has been entirely too long since I've seen my favorite girl, Amanda. How are you?"

"All the better now that I see you, Custis."

Taking Longarm by one hand she led him through the foyer to the formal parlor.

He very nearly balked in the doorway when he saw the parlor was already filled with guests. There were five ladies, each of them middle-aged or older, seated on the overstuffed furnishings, a tea table in the center of the room, a silver service arrayed on it.

"Ladies, this is Mr. Custis Long. He is a deputy United States marshal from Denver. Custis was my late husband Frank's dearest friend. And mine, too, I dare say. Please join us, Custis. Fanny, you can scoot over to make room for Custis, can't you? Thank you."

Amanda turned and motioned to the maid, who had followed them into the room. "Jessie, pour the marshal a cup of lemonade, please."

Trapped!

Longarm sat next to the elderly woman called Fanny— her name was descriptively apt for she had an overlarge butt—and accepted the silver demitasse cup of chilled lemonade.

"We were just discussing the novel *Ramona*, Custis. Have you read it?"

"Uh . . . no."

"No matter. Now where were we?"

Longarm sat politely and sipped at his lemonade while the conversation flowed around his ears . . . and over his head. He had no idea what these women were talking about. Nor did he care.

While the ladies talked and he pretended interest, injecting a wise nod or a spoken "that's interesting" every now and then, he had time to admire Mrs. Amanda Reese, widow of Frank Reese.

Amanda always introduced Longarm as her late husband's dear friend. In truth, Longarm had never met the man. He died—of something or other, Longarm had no idea what—before Longarm ever encountered Amanda.

He had met her by chance. Liked her and enjoyed her company.

The lady was still a very handsome woman with a full figure and delicate features. She was prim and proper and very much the socialite widow. And she had tits the size of bed pillows.

Longarm was contemplating those tits when he became aware that he was being spoken to. It took an effort of will for him to return from his reverie. "Pardon?"

"I was saying what a pleasure it is to meet a genuine deputy marshal of the sort we usually read about in the newspapers," one of the ladies was saying. He could not remember her name. Nor for that matter the names of any of the others save for Fanny.

The lady stood and extended her hand, and he climbed to his feet, aware now that the ladies were all standing and were saying their good-byes.

Longarm made the expected polite noises to see them off but lagged behind when Amanda herded them toward the door. He heard her say, "You may go now, Jessie. I won't need you again until morning. You can leave the dishes until then. Good night."

He heard the front door close and the sound of the maid's footsteps heading toward the back of the house. Then Amanda returned to the parlor.

She was laughing.

And unbuttoning the bodice of her dress.

Chapter 7

Magnificent! That was the only word to describe Amanda Reese's tits. If prizes were given out for tits, hers would surely qualify for the blue ribbon. Maybe a gold loving cup, too. They were large and firm with nipples the size of the demitasse cups the ladies had been drinking from. A thin tracery of blue veins showed beneath the pale skin.

Longarm took one of those nipples into his mouth and sucked. Hard. Amanda arched her back and moaned softly. Her tits were as sensitive as they were large, it seemed.

"During our meeting," Amanda confided, "all I could think about was having your cock again. So big and hard." She laughed. "And tasty."

"I have t' say, lady, that you are a champion when it comes t' sucking cock."

"I locked the doors, dear. No one can walk in on us this time."

Longarm laughed. There had been a time in a hotel room down in Denver when a maid came in to change the sheets and found the two of them spooned together face to crotch,

Longarm's cock plunging down Amanda's throat and his tongue probing her cunt.

Longarm was so startled that for a moment he stopped what he was doing. Amanda never faltered, however. She just kept on sucking until she had his come in her throat. Only then did she come up for air. Afterward she swore she had not noticed that they had company, but he was not sure that he believed her about that.

What he did believe about her was that Amanda Reese gave a man one hell of a roll in the hay.

"Come along, Custis. Let's quit teasing ourselves and get naked," Amanda said, rising and taking his hand.

She let her dress, already unbuttoned to the waist, fall to the floor so that she stood in the middle of the parlor wearing nothing but shoes, stockings, and her jewelry. It was not a bad combination, he thought. Amanda had a body that most women would kill for, full and shapely and firm.

Longarm unbuttoned and unbuckled as they went, dropping articles of clothing along the way so that by the time they reached Amanda's bedchamber he, too, was naked.

"Lovely," Amanda murmured as she dropped to her knees in front of him. She took a moment to admire his cock, erect and throbbing with anticipation by now, then cupped his balls in the palm of her hand while she slowly licked his dick up one side and down the other.

"Lovely," she said again, running her tongue around the head of his cock and inside his foreskin.

She continued licking and sucking him until he was close to coming, then she stood and moved backward to the four-poster bed. She lay on it and opened her legs to admit him into the wet heat of her pussy.

Longarm sank into the lady's body, filling her, pleasuring him. "Damn, woman. This feels fine."

"Glad to be of service," she said, laughing.

That was one of the many things Longarm liked about Amanda. She was a happy fuck, uninhibited and delighting in the pleasures she could give and those she received as well.

He plunged deep into her, one hand kneading one of those beautiful tits while he was inside her.

Then the heat began to build in his balls and he lost track of everything but the rising feel of his come until it exploded within Amanda's body.

Thinking his weight might be uncomfortable on top of her he started to roll away.

"No," she said, wrapping an arm around him to stop his motion. "Stay there, please. I like the feel of it inside me, if you don't mind."

Longarm settled down, cushioned by Amanda's tits, his face resting against her perfumed hair.

After a few minutes he dropped off to sleep like that.

Chapter 8

Longarm was back at the Graythorne Inn just as the sun was breaking the eastern horizon. He strode up to the desk and tapped the bell on the counter there. It drew a sleepy-eyed clerk out of the office.

"Yes, sir?"

"Mr. Hood, please."

"Sir, I don't think . . ."

"Mr. Hood, damnit, or I'll start through the place knockin' on doors until I find him myself," Longarm snarled. He was in no mood to be turned away this morning. Pleasant as the night had been, this was day. And there was work to be done.

"Sir, if you think . . . you wouldn't dare . . . sir, I will call the police if you keep this up."

Longarm pulled out his wallet, flipped it open to display his badge, and cleared his throat. "Like I said, bub. Knockin' on every door in the damn place."

"No, uh . . . no, please. I will see if . . ."

"You will *see* nothing. You will find the man and get his ass down here right damn now."

The clerk scampered out from behind his desk and up the stairs. Longarm followed close on his heels, not trusting the clerk to deliver C. Burton Hood ready to travel.

The man stopped at a door on the second floor and rather timidly tapped his knuckles on the door.

There was no response from inside the hotel room. The clerk lightly tapped the door a second time, then turned to Longarm with an apologetic shrug. "I'm sorry, sir, he . . ."

"Where's your key?"

"Sir?"

"Your key, man. You have one that will open any door in the place, don't you?"

"Yes, but . . ."

"Gimme it," Longarm demanded.

"But, sir, I can't . . ."

"You will give me the key right damn now," Longarm snapped, "or I'll put you in handcuffs an' haul your ass down to the city jail."

The clerk's resolve wilted and he meekly handed over the key. He looked like he wanted to escape but duty made him stay until Longarm had the door unlocked and returned the key to the man.

"You can go now," Longarm told him. The clerk bolted away as fast as he could without actually running.

Longarm sighed.

And pushed the door open.

Chapter 9

C. Burton Hood was sprawled across the hotel bed. He was young, thin, with a wild mop of curly hair. He was fully dressed and smelled of whiskey and perfume. Longarm had no quarrel with either of those, but it was well past the dawn now and Hood still lay there. Longarm was not sure if the man was asleep . . . or passed out. Either way, he needed to get up and get out. With assistance if need be.

"Wake up," Longarm snapped.

Hood's only response was a faint snore.

"Get up, damnit!" Longarm said, louder. He tugged Hood's wrist. That brought a mumbled "lemme 'lone" from the man.

Longarm was in no mood to stand there trying to cajole Hood onto his feet. He looked around, spotted the washstand. And the pitcher of fresh water beside the basin.

With a grunt, Longarm retrieved the pitcher, returned to the bedside, and dumped the entire contents—a good half gallon or more—onto Burt Hood's head.

That brought the young man up, fists swinging. Longarm blocked a roundhouse right hand and slapped Hood. Twice.

"Who the fuck . . . ?"

"Deputy United States Marshal Custis Long, that's who, and you were supposed to report to me last night. Now I find you sleeping off a drunk when you are supposed to be starting service as a deputy. Probational deputy, that is, an' judging from what I seen so far, boy, you aren't gonna make it in this service."

"Dep . . . oh. Yeah." Hood yawned. "I forgot." He shook his head, sending water flying in all directions, including onto Longarm, and muttered, "Jus' a minute," before tottering over to the washstand. He reached for the basin, realized it was empty and began looking for the pitcher, which Longarm was still holding. "Wait. I need . . . I need to . . . shit, I don't know what I need."

"You need to get your ass moving is what you need," Longarm snapped. "An' you need t' do it right damn now. You look like shit, but you're already dressed so grab your bag an' let's go. We got a train to catch."

"But I . . . but I."

"Now!" Longarm barked.

"Yes, sir." Hood began scurrying around the room, grabbing up articles of clothing and stuffing them into suitcases.

"How many bags you got, boy?" Longarm asked, his voice harsh.

"Oh, uh . . . four, actually."

"We aren't running a caravan here, kid. Pick one bag. Tell the hotel to hold the rest for you."

"But I can't possibly . . ."

"Do it!"

"Yes, sir."

"I'll be downstairs in the restaurant having coffee. Report to me there in eight minutes. I'm timing you." Longarm pulled out his Ingersoll railroad-grade watch and checked the exact time, then pushed it back into his vest pocket.

"Eight minutes. Any more an' I'll kick your ass from here t' the railroad station."

Longarm spun on his heels, tossed the empty water pitcher onto Hood's bed, and strode out of the room.

Chapter 10

It took Burt Hood twelve minutes to make it down to the dining room. But who was counting.

Longarm slipped the Ingersoll back into his vest pocket and nodded to the chair opposite his. "Sit down. Have some coffee. Something to eat, maybe. But mind you don't overspend for meals or anything else. Like fancy hotel rooms. We're traveling on the government's dime now, and you don't want to piss the boss off before you even meet him."

"Yes, sir. I'm, uh . . . I'm sorry. I've been . . . you know."

"Yeah, I know," Longarm said. "How old are you, anyway?"

"I'm twenty-one, sir."

Longarm grunted. C. Burton Hood was twenty-one? Longarm had been "older" at fourteen than Hood was now. But that was Hood's problem, not his.

They had a quick meal of porridge and coffee, both liberally laced with cream and sugar. Longarm paid. Marked the amount down in a notebook for Henry's sake, too.

"I have t' give you credit for one thing, Hood," Longarm

said. "You wear your gun so well hid that I can't spot it. In a shoulder holster, is it? Or d'you carry it in the small o' your back?"

"Gun, sir? I don't have a gun. Won't I be issued one by the marshals' service?"

Longarm spewed a mouthful of coffee and damn near choked. "You . . . don't have a gun? Really?"

Hood seemed mystified by the question. "No, sir. Am I supposed to have one?"

"Unless you figure t' immobilize your prisoners by drinking them under the table . . . yeah, kid. You have t' have a gun."

"Sorry, sir."

"Let me ask you somethin' else then. Can you *shoot* a gun?"

"Oh, yes, sir. I am quite proficient at shooting clay pigeons."

"You do know there's a heap o' difference between shooting a real live human person an' a lump o' formed clay, don't you? I mean . . . have you ever shot anything that's alive? A bird? A squirrel? Anything like that?"

"No, sir. Not exactly. But I did accompany my father on a hunting trip once. We didn't happen to catch anything, but it was fun being out in the wilderness with him." Hood laughed. "The kind of hunting I really enjoy is in the saloons and brothels out here."

"'Out here,'" Longarm repeated. "You aren't from 'out here,' Burt?"

"Oh, no, sir. I'm from Maryland."

"Do you want to be a deputy?" Longarm asked.

C. Burton Hood shrugged. And poured more cream onto his porridge.

This trip was starting off to be even worse than Longarm had imagined. "Tell you what, kid. We'll skip the morning train and take an afternoon westbound. This morning we got t' go buy you a pistol . . . you'll pay for it yourself, by the way . . . an' find an alley or somethin' where you can figure out how t' shoot it."

"Yes, sir. Whatever you say, sir."

Longarm finished his coffee, lighted a cheroot, and leaned back while he waited for Hood to finish breakfast.

Chapter 11

Longarm took Hood to a gunsmith that he knew would not try to cheat them and fitted the kid out with a cross-draw holster—"that's so's your gun won't fall out if you get in a storm atop a horse . . . or something"—and a Smith & Wesson break-top .44 along with two boxes of cartridges for the revolver.

"Is this the same as yours there?" Hood asked, pointing to the well-worn walnut grips on Longarm's Colt.

"No, but it's easier t' figure out, opening like it does. An' they're sturdy. The S and W is rugged as a rock. You can't hardly fuck 'em up." He managed a smile. "Even if you try."

"Can I shoot it a few times to get used to it?" Burt asked.

"Uh-huh. We'll step into the alley back here an' you can run through a cylinder. Kinda get the feel of it."

"All right. I'd like that."

Burt followed Longarm through a passage between buildings and into an alley where they found an assortment of broken crates, cast-off bottles, and such. "Won't people come running if we shoot a gun back here?"

Longarm shook his head. "Likely not. They'll think we're a couple drunks shooting at rats." He laughed. "Or they'll think we're a couple robbers back here shooting people. Either way they won't come looking."

He showed the kid how to load the Smith and had him dry fire it a few times to get the feel of it, then had him shoot at a piece of broken wood lying fifteen or twenty feet away.

"Isn't that awfully close?" Hood asked.

"Could put it closer actually. Real gunfights usually happen close enough you could damn near reach out an' touch the other guy with the muzzle o' your gun. Distance ain't a problem. An' another thing, forget everything you've ever heard about fast draws. A fast noise never killed nobody, so don't try an' be a gunslinger. If it comes to shooting, take your time. Aim. Hit the other son of a bitch while he's blowing holes in the air with his bullets. The mark of a good man with a gun is one who can keep his wits about him while there's bullets flying. So forget about speed. Take your time an' hit something." Longarm smiled. "Okay?"

C. Burton Hood grinned back at him. And felt the gutta-percha grips of the S&W that was riding high at his waist.

"One more question, kid," Longarm said.

"Yes, sir?"

"Can you ride a horse if we need to?"

This time it was Burt who smiled. "I've ridden to foxes most of my life. Cross-country eventing, too. I'm not so familiar with your big ol' western saddles. They seem awfully heavy to me. But I expect a horse here is pretty much the same as a horse back home."

Longarm clapped the young man on the shoulder and said, "Could be that you'll do, kid."

Chapter 12

"Our train leaves at one twenty?" Burt asked as they were walking back toward the depot.

"That's right," Longarm said. "We'll have lunch at a café across Front Street. Nice folks run it and the food is pretty good, too. D'you have something else in mind?"

"Not for lunch, but there's something I would like to do while we wait. If, um, if that's all right."

Longarm shrugged. "It's fine by me, just so's you aren't late." He smiled. "This time."

"I won't be. I promise." Burt wheeled and trotted away on his own. Longarm continued on toward the Union Pacific station. Fifteen minutes later Burt Hood joined him on the platform. He was carrying the one bag Longarm had allowed him. And he was smiling.

"Got everything done you needed to?" Longarm asked.

"I did," Burt said.

They had a quick lunch at the café Longarm recommended and boarded the westbound passenger coach on time. Once the train was in motion, Burt stood and said, "Would you like to go to the smoker?"

"Sure. We got better than an hour to kill," Longarm said.

Burt stood, took his bag down from the overhead rack and opened it.

"What . . . ?"

"You'll see," Burt said with a broad smile. He reached into his bag and brought out a quart bottle of Jespers Gold Label rye whiskey. "Something to help pass the time."

"Kid, is that what I think it is?" Longarm said.

"It's rye. I hope that is all right with you. They distill Jespers back home, and the Gold Label is their best. Sort of like a private stock, actually. Half of my friends' fathers work for Jespers, I think. I've been around it all my life. If you'd rather have something else . . ."

"Jespers. Boy, I knew there was some reason I like you. Now bring your friend along to the smoker car. You an' me will pull a cork and"—Longarm licked his lips—"have a taste o' that sweet nectar."

He became serious for a moment. "But we got t' be sober when we get to Rawlins. After all, we're here on official business."

"But it will be all right if we have a little drink between now and when we get to Rawlins, won't it?"

"Yes, kid. Oh, yes, indeed." Longarm practically trampled C. Burton Hood as they made their way, swaying from side to side, back to the smoking car.

Chapter 13

Longarm had a warm, comfortable glow in his belly when they stepped down off the UP passenger coach. Drinking Jespers Gold Label was drinking a warm cloud. And the kid grew up near the distillery. What luck.

"Supper now?" Burt asked, "Or should we get a room first?"

"Neither one. We're here t' work, remember. First thing, we check the schedule for a coach up to Thermopolis."

"We won't go tonight, will we?" Burt asked.

"If there's a night run to the north, we damn sure will," Longarm told him. "If I remember a'right, the stage line through here is Watson Express. We need t' find their office for the schedule."

Burt sighed. But he nodded understanding. "How do we—"

"We ask somebody, o' course," Longarm cut him off. "C'mon."

Twenty minutes later they were standing in front of the Watson facility. It was not calculated to inspire confidence.

The building looked more like a feed shed than a business office.

"This is . . . ?"

"Yeah," Longarm muttered.

Still, as far as stagecoaches went, Watson was the only game in town. Longarm pushed the door open and went inside. A thin man wearing an eyeshade and sleeve garters was dozing at a rolltop desk behind a low divider. The fellow roused himself away from whatever dreams or fantasies he might have been having to ask, "Help you fellas?"

"You have a coach going to Thermopolis tomorrow?" Longarm asked.

"Yes, sir. We make the run up twice per week. Up one day, back the next. That coach don't run on Sundays. Next northbound I got after this one isn't until next Monday. Do you want tickets?"

"We do," Longarm said.

"That will be seven dollars and eighty-five cents for each of you, and . . ."

Longarm stopped him with a display of his badge. "U.S. deputy marshals. You have a mail contract?"

"Yes, sir."

"In that case we ride free."

"Yes, sir. But you still need tickets."

"Two of them please," Longarm said.

Five minutes after that they were on the street again, looking for rooms and something to eat. Burt did not seem at all dismayed by the delay in their travel plans. If anything he seemed pleased by it.

Chapter 14

They took a pair of rooms at the Rest for the Wicked Hotel. If nothing else, Longarm loved the name of the place. And the rooms were reasonably clean if sparsely furnished and a little on a small side.

"Any choice between them?" Longarm asked the kid.

Burt shook his head and said, "Either will do. They seem to be the same."

"Then I'll take the one we're standin' in," Longarm said, dropping his carpetbag at the foot of the narrow bed.

Burt went through the connecting door to the other room and deposited his things there. When he returned he announced, "I'm hungry." He did not surprise Longarm in the least with that statement. "There's a restaurant in this hotel, isn't there?"

"Yeah, but I'm betting the grub there is only fair to middlin'. I'm going up the street to where I seen a likely looking café, but you can eat wherever you please. Just remember if you pay cash outta your pocket to get a receipt you can show Henry back at the office. He makes out the forms for reimbursement." Longarm smiled. "You want t' stay on the good side of Henry."

"I don't want to wait. I'm going to eat here," Burt told him.

"Suit yourself." Longarm took his time washing up and tidying himself after the train ride, then ambled downstairs and out onto the street. He noticed Burt bellied up to a table in the dining room. The youngster already had several plates in front of him. Longarm suspected he would need to let the kid know there were limits to the amounts Henry would approve on their expense reports.

It was dark by the time Longarm exited the Wicked Hotel, as he preferred to think of the place. The air had cooled down from the heat of the afternoon. It felt refreshing despite the smell of coal dust thanks to the railroad.

He paused on the hotel porch to light a cheroot and stood there for a few moments enjoying the feel of the evening before he ambled down the steps to street level and turned in the direction of the café he remembered seeing earlier.

All up and down the main street, a row of incandescent lightbulbs mounted on top of steel posts illuminated the business district. The effect of the dazzling white lights against the night sky was handsome in the extreme.

This assignment might not turn out to be as bad as Longarm feared when Billy gave it to him . . . shepherding some thieving little postal clerk and trying to break in a new kid at the same time. It sounded worse than it was proving to be.

In fact, Longarm was feeling rather good.

Then someone took a shot at him.

Chapter 15

The bullet smashed into the roof support post behind him and to his left, sending splinters flying but otherwise doing no damage. By the time the splinters hit the ground, Longarm was down there, too, .45 in hand and hat askew.

He had not seen the muzzle flash, which meant the shooter was somewhere behind him. But exactly where he had not the faintest idea.

He swiveled around in the dirt of the street and tried to make out where the shooter was. The possibilities were many. Too many. Every shadow or alley mouth could have concealed a man with a gun.

There was only the one shot. In a way, Longarm almost hoped there would be a second. At least then he would be able to see where the shooter was hiding. The bright flash of flame from a pistol or a rifle muzzle would be a dead giveaway. *Dead* giveaway indeed, Longarm thought. Although not, he hoped, applying to him.

He neither saw nor heard a thing that would suggest

where the shooter might be, and after several minutes of tense searching people began to appear on the street again.

Longarm stood, brushed himself off, and walked on—cautiously—toward that likely looking café, his stomach gurgling loudly. He could not decide if that was because he was so hungry . . . or because the moments of nervousness from being shot at had his stomach acids running wild.

Along about the time he was reaching for his second helping of fried potatoes, Longarm decided the bullet that struck so close to his head was nothing more than a stray shot, perhaps fired by a drunk or maybe it was someone trying to shoot an alley rat. It had nothing to do with him, he concluded.

Satisfied, he had those potatoes—he had scarcely tasted the first helping, his mind being occupied with thoughts of the shooting—and the rest of his meal, then paid and walked back to the Wicked.

He was more than normally cautious for only the first ten or fifteen yards. After that he relaxed and walked on as if nothing had happened earlier.

Back at the hotel he stripped and crawled into the narrow bed. The mattress was hard but the blankets were clean—there were no sheets, just the blankets and a scrawny excuse for a pillow—and he was asleep within moments.

He woke early as was his habit, got up and splashed some water on his face to get the sleep out of his eyes, then dressed. The last thing he did before leaving his room was to check his .45, making sure it was fully loaded and loose in his holster.

Not that he expected trouble. Exactly. But . . . a man never knew, as the previous evening had so clearly demonstrated.

When he was ready to face the day, Deputy Marshal

Custis Long opened the connecting door between his room and Burt Hood's.

He stopped. Gaped. Then laughed.

His young partner was squeezed onto the hotel's narrow bed along with two rather hefty young women. All three of them were naked as boiled eggs.

As best Longarm could determine around and beneath the girls' flow of unpinned hair—one blond and the other a redhead—the two females were busily attacking Burt's cock. One had his dick lodged deep in her mouth while the other was sucking his balls.

The amazement to Longarm was not so much what they were doing with one another—that seemed normal enough—as the fact that they could all fit onto that little bed at the same time without someone falling onto the floor.

Burt heard the door open and looked up from beneath his blanket of flesh. The kid moved a leg aside and peered over the top of a shapely calf.

"Good morning, Longarm. Care to join us?"

"Thanks, but I'll find my own pussy. Besides, kid, it's time you crawl out from under them females an' get yourself dressed. We got time to have some breakfast before that stage pulls out, but let me remind you. If we miss this northbound there won't be another till next week. So if you ain't ready in time, I'll go on without you."

"Don't you worry. I'll be there," Burt said.

"All right. Are you comin' down for breakfast?"

Burt grinned and reached down to squeeze the ass cheek of one of his women. "I'll finish here first if you don't mind."

"Suit yourself."

Longarm went downstairs and ate alone in the hotel dining room. He would have preferred walking down to the café where he'd had supper but he wanted Burt to be able to find him when the kid came down for breakfast.

As it happened, Burt never did show up to eat. And he barely made it to the Watson depot in time to climb aboard the stagecoach.

He was smiling hugely when he did get there.

Chapter 16

Thermopolis was not, in fact, a town. It was barely a village, the few residents providing for the needs of the tourists who came to wallow in mud from the naturally occurring hot springs. And even those "residents" were seasonal, coming back to their businesses in springtime and leaving in the fall for their permanent homes.

Longarm and Burt Hood crawled wearily down from the stagecoach and stretched. Longarm brought out a cheroot, bit the twist off, and lighted the slim cigar. Burt brought out his flask and shook it, hoping for a few more drops of the whiskey it had contained.

"I have to get this thing refilled before we start back," Burt said.

"First things first," Longarm said. "We have to find our prisoner an' arrange for our rooms overnight and tickets on the southbound coach tomorrow morning."

"Look, why don't you do that while I step over to that saloon and take care of this flask," Burt responded.

"You don't care about the rooms?"

"Of course I care about the rooms, but I know where they are gonna be. There's only that one hotel over there." He grinned. "Unless there's a whorehouse hidden around here somewhere. I could spend the night there and save the government the cost of my room."

"Now that's thoughtful of you, kid, but your whiskey an' your women can wait a bit while we find a place an' get settled in. Besides, we got to check in with whoever is handling the law here an' get a look at this . . . what was her name again?"

"Naomi Foster," Burt said.

"Oh, right. Foster." Longarm looked around. "I don't see a jail here or anything like an office where there might be a town marshal."

"So we find the rooms first and ask there?" Burt suggested.

"Sounds reasonable," Longarm said, picking up his well-worn carpetbag and heading toward the tall, ungainly hotel building. At least the sign out front claimed that it was a hotel. Longarm thought it looked more like a bunch of chicken coops stacked one on top of another.

While they walked he tried to spot anything that might look the least bit like a jail.

There was none.

Chapter 17

The hotel rooms made the Rest for the Wicked seem like the lap of luxury. The walls were canvas stretched over a rickety frame, and the beds were only wood frames with more canvas stretched over them. A single blanket was provided along with a thunder mug and a pair of hooks on the reasonably solid exterior wall. There was no lamp.

"Say, partner, how's about giving us each a lamp for those rooms," Longarm asked the desk man when he took the stairs—more like a sloping ladder than a staircase—back downstairs after dropping his carpetbag on the floor of his room.

The manager grunted, scowled, and pulled out a pair of candles that he handed over without ever actually speaking.

Longarm gave one of the candles to Burt and pocketed the other for the time being rather than risk life and limb by climbing back up to his room in the . . . it occurred to him that he had no idea what this hotel was called.

"What's the name of this place?" he asked the manager.

"Thermopolis," the man said.

"I know that. I mean what's the name of this hotel?"

"Don't have a name. Don't need one. Only hotel around here."

"What about your jail?"

"Don't have a jail."

"Surely you have a sheriff or a town marshal," Longarm said.

"Sort of," the hotel man said.

"What's that supposed t' mean?" Longarm asked.

"Got a fella that does that sort of thing. A little. See Earl over to the livery stable. Earl is close as we got to a town marshal."

Longarm opened his mouth to ask some more questions, but the hotel manager had already turned away and was poring over some papers on his desk, completely ignoring both Longarm and Burt Hood.

"Mister," Burt put in, loudly. "Mister, what about women? Do you have loose women in this town?"

"Not in this hotel, we don't," the manager said, swiveling around to eye Burt with glaring disapproval. "You try and bring some floozy in here and you will both be out on your asses. Mark my words. Out on your asses."

Longarm was not sure if the man meant that Burt and his woman would be thrown out—or in Burt's case, his women—or if he would toss out Longarm, too, if either one of them were to transgress the hotel rules.

"This is a family hotel. We got families for guests. Women, kids, no cheap women here, mind you, or out you go."

"Yes, sir," Burt said meekly. Then he turned his head and winked at Longarm.

"Where can we get something to eat?" Longarm asked.

The hotel manager ignored him. Apparently the man had used up his supply of available words, at least for the time being.

Longarm jerked his chin toward the street, and Burt followed him out into the afternoon heat.

Chapter 18

Supper was surprisingly good, cooked and served by a fat, cheerful Shoshone woman who knew her way around an oven. Halfway through the meal, Burt nudged Longarm and whispered, "Is that lady really an Indian?"

"Yeah, why?"

"I never saw one before," Burt admitted.

"Really? Then you never, uh, *been* with an Indian girl, eh?" Longarm returned his attention to his roast pork with rice and brown gravy.

"No, obviously not," Burt said. "Are they different?"

Longarm finished chewing, swallowed, then said, "Matter o' fact, they are. I figure they must be related somehow to the Chinese . . . you can kind o' see that when you look at 'em side by side, Injuns an' Chinese. They both got dark skin an' black hair, kinda flat noses and high cheekbones. Look at 'em together and you can see. But mostly you see it when you get one o' the women naked. Chinese or Injun either one, you can see it right off."

Burt laid his fork down and leaned closer to whisper, "How can you see?"

"The women," Longarm said, his voice low and his demeanor serious, "their pussy slits is sideways."

Burt sat up and gaped. "You're serious?"

"Dead serious, son," Longarm assured him.

"Sideways? Oh, my. Does it . . . does that feel different? When you get inside, I mean."

Longarm reached for a helping of fried apples. "Yeah, it feels different. Not bad, understand. But different. You get used to it, though."

"I'll be damned," Burt murmured. "Sideways."

"Uh-huh. Pass the rice, would you, please."

Throughout the rest of the meal, Burt Hood stared at the fat Indian woman. It was all Longarm could do to keep from bursting out laughing. But what the hell. Let the kid find out for himself. It was obvious he was aching to get some willing Shoshone girl's skirt up around her waist.

"Come along, kid. We need to check in with that fellow at the livery. Take a look at what we'll be taking back to Denver with us."

What passed for a livery in Thermopolis was basically a wagon park and a tack shed that pretended to be a barn. The Watson stagecoach that had carried them up from Rawlins was there, along with a number of other passenger rigs. The horses to pull them were in a series of corrals built behind the barn.

Stacks of hay had obviously been carted in from somewhere else. There certainly was no hay to cut around the village, which was as barren as the sands of Araby. But with hot springs and wild, pastel colors thrown in.

A middle-aged man, thin, wearing bib overalls and apparently nothing underneath, approached them at the entrance to the barn. "Sorry, gents. It's late. I'm not letting out any of my rigs tonight." He smiled, exposing yellow teeth. "I can put you down for first thing in the morning if you like."

"That's not what we're here about," Longarm told the hostler. He introduced himself and said, "We're here t' take the prisoner off your hands."

"It's about time," the liveryman said. "She's been costing us money, eating and everything."

"The government will reimburse you," Longarm assured him.

"Reim . . . what's that word mean?"

"It means the government will pay you back. You won't be out anything. I brought you some forms to fill out to get your money back."

"Is there a reward?"

Longarm grunted. "Don't know, actually. Nobody's mentioned anything like that to me. But you can claim it if there is one. I'll ask when we get back t' Denver."

"I'd sure like to get me a reward," the man said. "I'm the one that caught her. Seen a wanted poster with her likeness on it. We don't have a post office ourselves. Just the stagecoaches. They bring mail for us, and since I'm what passes for the law around here they always give any of those posters to me. That's how I seen her likeness. She admitted right off to who she is. I got her locked up over here. Come along. I'll show you."

"Can I ask you something?" Burt said.

"Sure. Ask anything you like."

"Are you an Indian?"

"No, sonny, I'm not, but this is Indian reservation land we're standing on. You'll find a right good many Injuns hereabouts. Civilized Injuns though." He laughed. "Your scalp is safe. Uh . . . probably. Come along now."

Chapter 19

The liveryman had Naomi Foster locked up in one of his rickety stalls. Literally locked up. He had wrapped chain around her waist—trace chain, Longarm suspected—and secured it with locks, Naomi at one end and a reasonably stout support post at the other.

Longarm could not see what she was wearing as she was covered head to toe by a linen duster that was several sizes too large for her. The man had supplied her with a water pitcher and a thunder mug. There was also a basket lined with a red-and-white-checked napkin and containing the crumbs of what must have been a slab of corn pone.

"Go find a mirror and stare at yourselves, you ugly sons of bitches," the delicate and most ladylike Miss Foster greeted them.

If she washed her face she might actually be pretty, Longarm thought. She was young, probably in her mid-twenties with shiny black hair, huge eyes—brown, he thought, but the light in the barn at this evening hour was not enough for him to be sure about that—pale, smooth skin. Her hair was done up in a bun. A good many strands were falling out. She had a small mouth, delicate features, and small hands. She was sitting slumped in a corner of the stall, but he got the impression that even standing at her full height she would be little more than a handful.

Or a mouthful. Which was not a subject it would be appropriate to raise with a prisoner, any prisoner, but especially one in his custody.

"We're your ticket out of here," Longarm told her. "Deputy United States marshals, sent here t' take you back to Denver. You'll stand trial there. You should know that it ain't up to us what happens to you except we're t' get you there."

"Go fuck yourselves," the girl spat.

"Are you always so charming?" Longarm asked.

"How old are you?" Burt asked.

Naomi ignored both questions. She turned her back to them and sat facing the wall.

"Sweet little thing, isn't she?" the hostler said.

"Is she always this pleasant?" Longarm wanted to know.

"Oh, she's on her good behavior this evening."

"Lord, help us," Longarm moaned.

"Unlock me, turnkey. These dumb bastards are taking me off to the gibbet," the girl snarled.

The hostler looked at Longarm and shrugged. "She talks like that. Half the time I can't understand what she's saying."

"Doesn't matter, I reckon," Longarm said.

"Not now that you're here to take her, it doesn't," the hostler said.

"Unlock me, bastard," Naomi screamed.

"In the morning," Longarm told her. "The southbound coach doesn't leave until morning."

"You sons of bitches have to get me a proper room. With

a tub. And something decent to eat. That's the law," she snapped back at him.

"Is that right?" Burt asked. "Do we have to do that?"

"Hell, no," Longarm told him. "She'll stay locked up right here until we're ready for the stage t' leave." He looked down at the liveryman, who was a good head shorter, and said, "Come along, mister. I'll get you those papers to fill out so's you can get paid back for what you put out on her."

"Ten cents a damn day," Naomi yelled. "He didn't feed me any better than a dime a day."

Longarm tipped his hat in her direction and politely said, "We'll try an' go fifteen cents till we get you down to Denver."

"Bastard. Cocksucker."

Longarm ignored the girl and motioned for Burt to come along.

Chapter 20

"There doesn't seem t' be much in the way of nightlife around here," Longarm said as they ambled along what passed for a street in the tiny collection of buildings, "but there's a gentlemen's club over there. Likely we can get a drink there. Care t' join me?"

"Yes, sir," Burt said enthusiastically.

The saloon—which insisted it was a gentlemen's club and not some ordinary saloon—did indeed offer liquor. Very good liquor, in fact. Very *expensive* liquor.

"Whew!" Longarm complained. "This piss is way the hell above a deputy marshal's salary. Reckon I'll have the one shot o' whatever their cheapest rye is an' call it a night."

"Don't be silly," Burt said. "I'm pretty well fixed." He turned his head and called, "Barkeep. A bottle of Jespers Gold Label, please. And two glasses."

"Yes, sir. coming right up."

Burt paid the exorbitant price of fifteen dollars for the one bottle and did not even wince.

When they were on their second glasses of the smooth

rye whiskey, an extraordinarily pretty Indian girl targeted Burt—who was young and handsome and had money—as her evening partner. Her flashing eyes and subtle display of pretty legs made her interest abundantly clear.

There was a good deal that Custis Long could teach C. Burton Hood about law enforcement, but the youngster had hit his stride already when it came to women. He was just plain randy. And ready.

Burt slid his chair back from the table. "If you will excuse me, Longarm, I think I'm going to check on whether they really are slanted sideways."

It took Longarm a moment to remember what that comment was about. Then he laughed. "Go ahead. Just be there when that stage pulls out in the mornin'."

"Yes, sir. But you, um, don't care what I do in the meantime?"

"Go. Have fun."

Burt flashed a grin his way and took off practically at a high lope to snag the little Indian whore before someone else got to her.

Longarm had another drink of the wonderful rye, then picked up his bottle and glass and carried them to a table where four men—coachmen rather than dandies to judge by their dress—were playing some low-stakes poker.

"Got room for a fifth, gents?"

"Drag over a chair, mister."

Burt had found his entertainment for the evening. Now so had Longarm. He pulled out a cheroot, lighted it, and declared that all was well with the world.

Chapter 21

"What the *hell* has happened to you?" Longarm barked, marveling at the state Burt seemed to be in.

The young man had no hat, no coat, no gun belt, and no boots. His right-hand trousers pocket had been ripped so bad that his thigh was showing through the gap.

Burt shook his head sadly. "The worst of it is that I never got to see that sideways pussy."

"How many o' them was there?" Longarm asked.

"Darned if I'd know, sir. She had her shirt open and her titties showing. I felt . . . it was more like I could hear it inside my head than I could feel it. Then the next thing I knew I was on the floor with my face in some cold puke and it was morning. I rinsed off a little in a horse trough down the street, and, well, here I am."

"Did she offer you a drink?"

"Yes, sir, but I didn't take it. I knew it wouldn't be near as good as the Jespers, so I left it alone. I guess it would have had something in it to knock me out easy, huh?"

"Oh, I'd say that was a pretty good guess. A little late,

but a good guess nonetheless. So they couldn't drug you, and bashed you on the head instead. Turn around and let me see."

Longarm fingered through Burt's hair. There was a lump the size of a duck egg rising on top of his crown. "You're damn lucky they didn't kill you. A whack on the head can do that, y'know. Likely your hat cushioned the blow a mite." Longarm shook his head in rapt wonder. Then he smiled. "Some deputy, you are, kid. A lawman from way back. At least you didn't have a badge for them t' steal. Now that would've been embrassing."

"Marshal, they took every cent I had on me. *Every cent.* What am I going to do now?"

"I expect you're gonna come with me to have break-fast . . . meals are expense account items, y'know, so whatever I spend I'll get back once we're home in Denver," Longarm said.

"But that is another thing. When we do get to Denver, I won't have a penny then, either. I'll need to find a room. Buy a gun and a hat and all that kind of stuff."

"You didn't leave anything hidden inside your bag? No sort of emergency funds?"

"No," Burt said. "I was afraid if I left money untended it wouldn't be there when I got back."

"So you carried it all with you, and . . ."

"Yes, sir. And now this."

Longarm sighed. "Well, come along with me. We'll have a quick bite o' breakfast, then go get the Foster girl. Fortunately I have our tickets safe in my pocket here."

"I'm sorry, sir, I . . ."

"You learned a lesson is what you did," Longarm said.

"But I didn't even get so much as a peep at that crossways pussy. I really wanted to see that."

"You'll have plenty of opportunity for that later on."

"Yes, sir. Thank you for not hollering at me."

"Hell, kid, you been punished enough without me piling onto you, too. Now come along. If we miss this coach, there won't be another until Tuesday. We . . . kid, are you all right?"

But Burt had gone suddenly pale. His eyes rolled up in his head and he toppled forward into Longarm's arms. Longarm eased him down to the floorboards and ran downstairs to see if there was a doctor anywhere in the village.

Chapter 22

"We don't have a doctor here," a gentleman at the hotel said, a man Longarm had not seen before. "We do have . . . I'm not sure I should even mention it."

"Go ahead. Whatever it is, you can at least say it," Longarm urged.

"He isn't a doctor. Not even a horse doc. But he's . . . the truth is that he's a shaman."

"A witch doctor?" Longarm blurted.

"No, a shaman. A Shoshone shaman. He's good. I've seen him do marvelous things. Almost miraculous. Let me call him for the young man."

"All right. Shit, I don't know what else t' do," Longarm said.

The gentleman nodded and hurried away. Longarm went back upstairs to sit with Burt, although he did not know what good he could do there if the young man went into convulsions or something.

Burt was pale and still completely limp. His breathing was shallow and his color almost nonexistent.

After only a few minutes Longarm heard the stomp of running footsteps on the stairs. He looked up to welcome the shaman. And blinked. The Indian was the same skinny, long-haired youngster, probably not yet out of his teens, who had been selling trinkets to the tourists outside the saloon the evening before.

He was dressed in beaded buckskins, a breechclout, leggings, and a vest, all of them decorated with colored porcupine quills. His hair hung in feathered braids. Longarm half expected to see him wearing some paint, but he did not. His skin was the color of walnuts and his eyes like shards of obsidian.

"Are you . . . ?"

"I am," the shaman said. "My name is Ben." He smiled, his dark eyes shining. "You don't want to know my true name. It would only tie your tongue into knots."

"Ben it is then. My name is Custis."

"And the patient?"

"His name is Burt."

"That is short for Bertram?"

"For Burton," Longarm said. "Does it make a difference?"

Ben shrugged. "Perhaps. Excuse me now, please." He dropped to his knees and examined Burt's head, clucking a little at what he found there. Then he pursed his lips and rocked back on his heels.

Longarm was expecting . . . hell, he did not know what he was expecting, really.

What Ben did was to break into a low, throaty song, a sort of chant. While he was singing, the shaman ran his hands over Burt's head, then his belly, then his chest and back to his head. Every once in a while he would look up, sometimes clap his hands, but always he was singing.

Longarm could not make out any of the words beyond

an occasional mention that he thought was "Burton." Past that he understood nothing, and the fleeting mentions that he thought were the patient's name might well have been something else entirely.

After a good ten minutes of this, Ben grunted and stood up. "We can move him to the bed now."

"All right."

Ben and the hotel man helped Longarm pick Burt up and transfer him, still out cold, onto the bed. They happened to be in Longarm's room, but that did not matter.

Longarm had to admit that Burt's color was somewhat better now. His cheeks did not seem quite so deathly pale, and his breathing was deeper, not yet normal but definitely better.

"Let him sleep," Ben said. "When he wakes he will remember dreams that will be strange to him, but he will be well. Keep him in bed for a day or two. I will bring marrow bones for him." Ben nodded. "Buffalo. Very good. Very rich. Let him eat of the marrow. It will be good for him. And no whiskey for at least two days."

"Two days, right." Not that that mattered really. By now they had already missed the southbound stagecoach, and there would not be another until Tuesday on the turnaround from the Monday northbound.

"What do I owe you for the, um, professional services, Ben?"

"I do not take money for the gift I have been given. If I accepted payment, the gift would be taken away."

"Is it all right if I thank you, then?" Longarm asked.

Ben's smile flashed. "That would be very nice."

"In that case, friend, I thank you most truly."

After the shaman left, Longarm stood for a time looking down at his partner. Burt's breathing was deep and steady and his color was almost completely back.

Of course it was entirely possible that the same thing would have occurred if no one had done anything, if Long-arm had just allowed Burt to lie there on the floor until he felt better.

That was something he would never know.

Chapter 23

Longarm looked up from the week-old Salt Lake City newspaper he was reading. "Where d'you think you're going, kid?"

"I just want to get up and move around a little. I've been lying in this bed all day," Burt said.

Longarm shook his head. "The doctor said two days. You stay where you are. If you need anything, I'll bring it to you." He had not gotten around to mentioning that the "doctor" was a shaman. He figured that bit of information could wait until Burt was better. And he did seem to be on the mend.

"Then slide the thunder mug over here, would you? I have to take a piss," Burt said.

"It's underneath your bed. You can reach it."

"Look, you've been cooped up in here with me all day except for meals. Why don't you take the evening off. Go play some cards. Or get laid. Or something," Burt said.

"How do you feel?"

"Groggy," Burt said, "but not really bad. My vision is

clearing up. I'm still a little dizzy. If you mean would I jump out of bed and go somewhere if you aren't here to ride herd on me, no; I'm not going anywhere for a while. Go on. I appreciate you watching out for me, but there is no need for both of us to go mad with boredom. Besides, shouldn't you go check on the prisoner?"

"Shit, you're actually making sense." Longarm smiled. "For a change." He stood, his knee joints cracking, and rubbed his face. "You're sure you're all right?"

"I'm fine."

"You won't get out of bed?"

"I promise," Burt said.

Longarm grunted. And reached for his hat. "I'll just take a little sashay around what town there is out there. I won't be long."

"Take your time."

The warm, dry air felt good after being inside virtually all day long. Longarm paused outside the hotel to light a cheroot, then walked over to the livery where Naomi Foster spat at him and cussed him up one side and down the other.

"It's good to see you feelin' so chipper," he told her, more amused than he was offended.

"Get that see-gar out of my barn. You want to burn the place down?" the hostler—whose name, he had learned, was Hank Wiggins—yelled from the back of the alley that ran between the stalls.

"If the fire would take this one with it, it might not be such a bad thing," Longarm said.

Wiggins laughed. The girl shouted, "Fuck you."

Longarm grinned. "You haven't lost any o' your delicate charms," he told the girl. He had brought her some water and a towel he swiped from the hotel. She had cleaned herself up a little and fastened her hair up. Except for her choice of language she was quite pretty.

He touched the brim of his Stetson toward Wiggins to acknowledge the man's concerns about fire danger, then took himself and the offending cigar out of the livery.

He ambled on toward the gentlemen's club, passing the boyish-looking shaman on the way and giving Ben a silent salute as well. He would have stopped to chat with the young Shoshone except there was a gaggle of tourists gathered around the young man admiring the trinkets he had for sale, and Longarm did not want to ruin Ben's chances to earn a profit.

Inside the saloon he saw the usual table of coachmen at a card table. One of the men noticed Longarm and motioned for him to join them.

Longarm stopped first at the bar for a drink, which he carried to the card table with him.

"Deal me in, gents," he said, taking the offered chair.

An hour or so later a man tried to kill him.

Chapter 24

Longarm glanced up when the door opened. A small, swarthy man, pudgy, wearing a black broadcloth suit and a wide-brimmed, vaquero-style hat came into the saloon. He seemed nervous, and instead of moving to the bar for a drink or seeking out one of the games of chance, the fellow stood just inside the doorway looking over the crowd.

Finally his attention locked onto Longarm. He took two steps forward onto the gaming floor and reached under his coat.

The man had done nothing to draw attention to himself, but his demeanor did that for him.

The lawman's instincts focused his attention on the man—Indian, perhaps, or Mexican, either way he seemed out of place—as he drew a large caliber revolver from beneath his coat.

Longarm was more curious than alarmed.

Until the SOB pointed his revolver in Longarm's direction and hauled the hammer back.

Longarm reacted without taking time to think or to wonder. His own .45 came into his hand even as he was throwing himself out of his chair. He landed on the floor and rolled.

The assailant's pistol belched smoke and flame, and the man who had been sitting beside Longarm at the poker table screamed in pain.

Longarm was more accurate with his return fire. His first bullet struck the shooter high in the chest.

The man staggered backward, and Longarm shot him again, this time hitting him in the belly.

He fell, his revolver still in hand.

The patrons in the saloon scattered like a flock of sheep escaping a pair of wolves.

The smoke in the room was so thick it was difficult to see, and in such close quarters the normally pleasant scent of gun smoke had become a heavy, acrid stink.

Longarm picked himself up off the floor, Colt still in hand. He looked around, cautiously, but there appeared to be no other danger. He shoved the .45 back into its leather and approached the dying man.

"Why?" he asked, kneeling beside the vaquero. "Why?"

"The money, senor," the man whispered. Moments later he was dead.

Money? What fucking money was he talking about, Longarm wondered.

Finally he concluded the incident had to be—simply *had* to be—a matter of mistaken identity. No one he knew of had reason to hire a killer to come after him.

At least . . . he did not think anyone did.

"If it's all the same to you, mister," one of the card-playing coachmen said, "we're done for tonight, so you can move along, please." Another of his former card partners was holding a handkerchief to a gash in his upper arm where the shooter's bullet had drawn blood.

Longarm grunted an acknowledgment of his dismissal, then headed back to the hotel. He had to clean his Colt tonight anyway.

Chapter 25

"Sorry, kid, I couldn't find any shoes or boots for sale around here, but I did get this pair o' genuine, tourist-grade, fancy beaded Injun moccasins for you. They're better than goin' barefoot." Longarm grinned. "But not much."

"Did you find a pistol for me to carry?" Burt Hood asked hopefully.

Longarm shook his head. "Nope, no pistol. You'll just have t' wait until we get south to a proper town. Not that I know what you'd use to buy it with even if we did find one."

"I can send a telegram to my father," Burt said. "He can wire some money to me. Enough to carry me through until I get paid anyway."

"You can send a wire from Rawlins and have the money sent to you in Denver."

"Yes, sir. I'll do it that way then."

"Will you be up to traveling in the morning?" Longarm asked.

"Yes, I'm fine now. Except for the humiliation. That still hurts, but otherwise I'm ready to go."

"All right. We'll be up extra early in the morning, have a quick breakfast, an' go over to the livery to collect our prisoner. The stage leaves at seven thirty so there's no time t' waste."

"Don't worry. I'll be ready," Burt assured him.

Longarm went downstairs and out onto the hotel porch to smoke a last cheroot, then went up to bed.

He woke before dawn the next morning and checked on Burt who, good to his word, was already up and dressed.

They had breakfast then walked over to the livery stable. There was no sign of Wiggins, but the hostler had already given Longarm a key to the lock on Naomi Foster's chains.

"What do you bastards want?" she snarled.

"Time to go meet your punishment," Longarm told her, "but t' tell you the truth, I don't want to hear you run your mouth the whole way t' Denver. So I'll make you a deal. You keep your mouth shut an' I'll handcuff your wrists in front. That won't be quite as miserable as putting them behind your back.

"If you insist on bitching an' moaning all the while, I'll truss you up like a calf bein' led to the fire an' pack you on top o' the coach where you won't be such a bother. Act nice an' you can ride inside like a regular passenger. Either way you'll be in handcuffs."

The girl gave him a look that was pure venom. But she kept her mouth closed.

Longarm nodded, knelt, and secured the handcuffs to her wrists but in front of her body where she at least had a little freedom of movement.

"Burt," he said, "you're in charge o' watching over the prisoner. See that she don't run nor do anything stupid. Treat her like a human person. Unless she proves she don't belong in polite company, in which case you treat her like a piece o' baggage."

"Yes, sir."

"All right now. Let's go catch that southbound coach before we get left behind for another two days."

Chapter 26

"I have to take a piss."

The other two passengers, a pair of schoolteachers from Wisconsin, gasped at Naomi's shocking language. Burt looked at Longarm for guidance about what to do in this situation.

"We'll stop at a relay station in another half hour or so," Longarm said. "You can hold it until then."

The tourists sniffed and looked away. Naomi looked at the women, who were probably in their forties, and laughed. It was obvious that she enjoyed shocking them like that.

From the driving box above the coach they could hear the jehu call "whoa" to his team as they lurched out of a dry creek bed onto reasonably level ground.

Longarm looked at his watch. He was sure they were not due to make a stop for that half hour or so, but the wildly rocking coach came to a complete halt.

"We aren't carrying a strongbox," he heard the driver say.

Another voice said something that Longarm could not make out. Then the driver said, "Go to hell, you."

There was the crack of a gunshot. Then another, followed by the wet thud of a large body falling and the coach rocked from side to side.

Longarm palmed his .45 and shoved the coach door open. A third gunshot sounded, and a small hole appeared in the polished wood veneer of the coach door.

The two tourist women screamed. Burt Hood, to his credit, flung himself over Naomi Foster to shield her from the shooting.

Longarm took a deep breath, then threw himself out of the open doorway, hit the ground, and immediately rolled aside while he searched for a target.

He heard a flurry of hoofbeats from the far side of the coach. Whoever the shooter was he got out of the way before Longarm had time to find a target and shoot.

One of the horses was down in the traces and the driver was slumped into the bottom of the driving box.

Longarm quickly climbed up the side of the coach to reach the box. The driver was dead, a bullet hole through his left temple.

"Shit," Longarm mumbled under his breath.

The man had a pistol strapped at his waist. Longarm unbuckled the dead man's gun belt and pulled it out from under his body. He had never gotten his pistol out of the leather.

Longarm checked the man's pockets, but his gun belt did not have cartridge loops and he carried no extra cartridges in his pockets. The revolver was an Iver Johnson .38 with five cartridges in the cylinder. And no spares. Better than nothing, he thought.

Even with the advantage of height there was no sign of whoever it was who killed the coach driver.

"Leave her, Burt, an' come help me," Longarm called. When Burt stepped out Longarm handed him the dead driver's gun belt. "Do you want his boots, too?"

Burt made a sour face and shook his head. "I . . . I don't think so. I'd feel funny about wearing those."

"Suit yourself. Now help me cut that dead horse out o' the harness."

"Can we continue with just three horses?" Burt asked.

"Hell, kid, I don't see as we got much choice about that. We go on with three horses or we don't go on at all."

"All right then, let's get to it."

Between them they unhooked the dead animal from the harness. Longarm took the off leader, now the only leader, by the bit and backed it—and the coach—until they were clear of the dead horse.

"We'll put the driver back in the luggage boot," Longarm said.

"Yes, sir." Burt climbed into the box and lowered the dead man to Longarm, who carried him to the back of the coach.

They had to transfer some luggage to the roof to make room for the driver's body. Then Longarm fastened closed the leather covered boot and walked toward the front of the outfit.

From somewhere off to the left he heard the boom of a rifle shot and again there was the dull thump of a falling body.

Chapter 27

"Aw, crap," Longarm mumbled when he saw what the damage was. The near wheeler was down in the traces now. The horse was not dead. Yet. But it was dying, its breath ragged and shallow.

Burt came running up to the front of the coach. The youngster stopped and gaped. "Can we . . . ?"

"Yeah. Maybe," Longarm answered, not waiting for Burt to finish his question. "But we got a problem here. If we back up any more, the coach will slip down into that arroyo we just came out of, and I doubt we could get it out again with just the two horses."

"Then what . . . ?"

A hundred yards or so to the east there was a puff of thin white smoke and a moment later the smack of a bullet into flesh. The near leader went to its knees.

"Never mind," Burt said.

"Kid, this one horse can't pull a Concord by its lonesome. From here we . . ."

The distant rifleman fired again and the last remaining horse died with a bullet in its brain.

"Son of a bitch can shoot," Longarm said.

"What does he want?" Burt asked.

Back in the stagecoach the two tourists were wailing. Naomi Foster simply sat, placid for a change.

Longarm glanced in her direction and said, "Could be the guy wants to free our prisoner, though I don't remember bein' told anything about her having a boyfriend or a protector. Apart from her"—he shrugged—"I can't think of much o' anything."

Burt peeped around the front of the now-stationary coach. "I can't see him," he said.

"He's down in that dry creek bed out there. Bastard knows we can't touch him with pistol fire. Not at that range. We could burn up all the ammunition we got an' likely not come closer than a couple feet while him with his rifle can pepper us as much as he likes."

"What do we do now?" Burt asked.

"We wait," Longarm said. "We calm the women down, an' we wait. Sooner or later he'll get tired o' this long-range shit an' get around to doing whatever it is he came here for."

Burt shuddered. He was pale and obviously frightened, but he went back to the passenger cabin and climbed inside. Longarm could hear him trying to soothe the women.

As for himself, Longarm perched on the door sill of the coach, crossed his legs, and lighted a cheroot.

Chapter 28

"You certainly look calm enough," Burt said, his voice a little shaky.

"It'll be time t' worry soon enough," Longarm said. "There's no need rushing things."

"Mr. Long."

"Yes, ma'am," he answered the Wisconsin schoolteacher.

"Are we to die here?"

He smiled at her. "I don't think so. I'm not sure what that fella out there has in mind, but right now he's just playing with us. His rifle could punch holes in the sides o' this coach if he wanted to. See there?" He pointed to the one bullet hole that had driven through the side of the coach earlier. "That's what I mean."

"Are we going to die?" the other tourist asked.

"O' course we are gonna die," Longarm said, laughing. "Everyone does sooner or later. The point is t' make sure that won't be real soon."

"I just wish . . ."

"Yeah." Longarm settled back, his head wreathed with smoke from his cigar.

After a time Burt mused, "To tell you the truth, Longarm, this is not how I envisioned a deputy's work, this being shot at and . . . everything."

"You thought of it as something of a lark?" Longarm asked.

"I suppose I did, yes."

"It can get real serious, kid." He grinned. "Like now, for instance." He noticed that Burt's hands were shaking and he kept swallowing even though he had nothing in his mouth to get rid of.

Nothing, that is, until he bolted out of the coach, dropped to his knees, and puked onto the hard-baked, barren soil of the badlands south of Thermopolis.

Longarm looked away and did not comment when Burt rather sheepishly crawled back inside the coach.

"If that's some pal of yours out there," Longarm said to Naomi Foster, "you and him both should know that we ain't turning you loose no matter how many holes he drills through this coach nor however many horses he wants t' kill."

Naomi gave him a look that was clearly frightened. She shuddered and said, "That is no friend of mine. He could have hit any one of us when he shot through the coach like that, me included."

Longarm grunted. But it was, in fact, true. The rifleman had demonstrated his ability to turn the Concord into Swiss cheese if he wanted. That he had not hit anyone, Naomi included, was a matter of chance, not skill.

The fact that he was not continuing to riddle the vehicle with bullets was a matter that he obviously understood but about which Longarm had no clue.

"I'm thirsty," one of the tourists complained. Quickly her companion began to whine as well.

Longarm looked at Naomi, expecting her to chime in with complaints of her own, but she was silent.

"I could drop back into that gulch or whatever you call it," Burt offered.

"Arroyo," Longarm said. "It's an arroyo."

"Yes, well, whatever it is, there might be water in the bottom of it. I could slip over there and take a look."

Longarm shook his head. "I don't want you t' do that, kid. I got something in mind for that arroyo, an' I don't want us calling attention to it now. But if anybody's hungry, we could maybe slice some chunks o' meat off one of those horses. I think we could reach them without exposing ourselves to the gunman."

No one took him up on the offer.

Chapter 29

The breeze died in mid-afternoon and the heat became oppressive, all of them suffering for the lack of water. The tourists bitched until they ran out of interest in it. Naomi remained silent except for to ask that her handcuffs be removed for the time being. She coped with the heat by unbuttoning the front of her dress and fanning herself. Longarm thought Burt's eyes were going to pop out of his skull from staring at the girl while pretending to look elsewhere. But then she was, he had to admit, rather good looking.

Once every half hour or so the distant rifleman would fire a round but always aiming high, chipping splinters off the roof of the coach but never shooting low enough that he risked hitting any of the passengers.

"Why is he doing that?" Burt asked after one shot clanged off the metal luggage rack.

"Showin' us he's still there," Longarm said. "He wants us t' know he hasn't gone nowhere."

"What are we going to do, Marshal? Surely you can do

something," one of the schoolteachers said late in the afternoon. "You are the law, after all."

"Ma'am, with all due respect, I ain't standing out there an' getting my ass shot off just to prove I'm brave. I got something in mind, but we got t' wait until dark or it won't work."

"What about those horses, Marshal?"

"They're dead, ma'am, an' there's nothing any amount of law can do t' change that," Longarm said.

A little while later Naomi climbed down from the coach and nestled on the ground tucked in close beside Burt. When Longarm raised an eyebrow she said, "I feel safer this way."

He thought it a trifle odd that she would be feeling that way this late in the day, but then he could not gauge her feelings nor know what was in her mind.

"If anybody's hungry," he said near sundown, "you'd best speak up now before that horsemeat spoils. That won't take long, hot as it's been. Anybody want some?"

"How . . . how would you cook it," the schoolteacher named Gladys asked timidly.

"No way t' cook it, ma'am. What's best is you just cut it in thin strips an' eat it the way it comes."

The woman frowned and turned her face away. Longarm assumed that was a "no" to his question.

He got on his belly and crawled over to the off wheeler, lying flat so the horse's body shielded him from the rifleman. He had a little difficulty slicing through the tough hide but the meat came away easily enough, dark red and sticky with coagulated blood.

"How does it taste?" Burt asked.

"Like shit, but it fills the hole in your belly," Longarm said. "Want some?"

"No, thanks."

The girl, Naomi, surprised him again. She squirmed a little but said, "I'll take some."

Longarm sliced off a chunk of the raw horsemeat and handed it to the girl. She took it and began to chew. If she found the flavor to be distasteful, she did not show it.

Overhead another of the rifleman's bullets droned past like a monstrous bumblebee.

Longarm leaned against a wagon wheel and carefully wiped his hands on his trousers.

"You about ready for some fun?" he asked Burt.

"What kind?"

"Oh, I got a little job for you t' do, deputy," he said, emphasizing the word "deputy" to remind Burt of his duty.

"Yes, sir."

"Then let's see can we get this little party started."

Chapter 30

"Burt, you are gonna make a little noise. I want you t' crawl up near the head of the off leader, an' make some noise. I don't want you to be obvious about it. I mean, not too much noise. But enough t' be heard. Maybe unhook a trace chain an' let it rattle some. Like I say, noise but not loud. Can you do that?" Longarm said.

"Yes, sir, I can do that, but what will you be doing?"

"I'll be going in the other direction."

Burt Hood raised an eyebrow, but Longarm did not elaborate on his plan. After a moment Burt asked, "Can I take the girl with me? She seems to be comforted by being close to someone."

Longarm said, "Take her with you if you wish. Matter o' fact it's probably a good idea to keep her close so's you can keep an eye on her."

"When, um, when should I start?" Burt asked.

"Now would be fine," Longarm said, then turning to the schoolteachers he added, "If you ladies want t' wail a little

more, now would be the time to do it. Sniffle an' blubber all
you like."

If either heard him, they gave no sign of it. But that was
all right, too, he thought. He was not counting on the schoolteachers' help.

Longarm stayed where he was until Burt and the girl
crawled out toward the front of what had been the team of
four horses. He was not sure exactly what they were doing
out there but he could hear . . . something. Something muf-
fled and indistinct. Perfect.

Once the rifleman's interest should have shifted toward
the front of the dead team—or so Longarm fervented hoped
it was anyway—he slipped over the drop into the arroyo the
coach had climbed out of just before the ambush.

The wall of the arroyo was no more than four feet high,
but that was enough to provide him with some cover from
the rifleman's bullets. More importantly, the soft, loose sand
at the bottom provided him with silence.

Crouching low to avoid being seen, Longarm palmed
his .45 and made his way southeast along the arroyo floor
toward the unknown gunman's hiding place.

Sixty yards on Longarm smiled as the rifleman fired once
more, his muzzle flash pinpointing his position.

Moving carefully, Longarm crept within eight or ten
yards from the place where he had seen that muzzle flash.

He held his Colt by the barrel long enough to wipe his
palm on his trousers, then resumed his grip on the .45, took
a deep breath, and stood up.

In the dim light of the stars overhead he could see a dark
shape kneeling in an arroyo that intersected the cut where
Longarm was hiding.

He took aim on the figure before he spoke.

"You're under arrest, cocksucker," he announced in a
loud, firm voice. Then immediately, without waiting for a

response, he added, "Stop or I'll shoot. Hands up. Don't move."

He would not normally have gone through that stupid litany of instruction, but Billy Vail had said he should do everything strictly by the rule book so as to give Burt a head start on legal procedure.

The result of all the palaver was just about what he expected. The rifleman swiveled around to face toward the sudden voice in the night. And swung the barrel of his rifle in that direction when he did so.

Longarm did not wait for the man to shoot. His .45 bucked and spat flame and a solid lead slug crashed into the rifleman's chest.

"Ay, madre!" the gunman blurted before he collapsed in the dirt where he had been hiding.

Longarm was too old a hand and too wise in the way of gunfights to immediately expose himself by rushing forward to observe the effect his bullet had. Instead he stayed where he was and listened to the dying man's breathing, welling blood making the sound a series of moist gurgles that gradually lessened and finally disappeared altogether.

Only then did Longarm very cautiously move into the shallow wash where the gunman had made his ambush.

The rifleman was still alive, if barely, and was dying—no surprise there—but it was obvious from his sombrero that he was another Mexican.

Before he did anything else, Longarm plucked the rifle away from the man. It was one of the heavier Winchester models firing a large-caliber cartridge suitable for elk or buffalo or the like. The fellow had no revolver.

"Why?" Longarm asked. "Why'd you shoot high like that?"

The Mexican looked at him, his breathing very shallow, then whispered, "Ladies. Di'n wan . . ."

"Didn't want to shoot the ladies?" Longarm asked.

The man nodded.

And died, the light going out of his eyes and his last breath sagging from his deflating body.

Longarm grunted softly. The man had enough conscience that he did not want to shoot the women. But it seemed to have been quite all right, highly desirable even, for him to shoot the men. Strange!

Then he smiled. He could still hear the slow rustling of . . . something, he was not sure what . . . from the direction of the coach. Burt and the girl were still doing something there.

Standing and taking a deep breath he called to them, "It's all right now. All over an' done with."

Even so they kept on making their noises until he was almost back to the stalled coach.

Chapter 31

Longarm climbed out of the arroyo and walked back to the stagecoach across the flat. He stumbled once on an unseen rock and almost dropped the rifle. He had not wanted to leave a weapon lying loose for just anyone to find.

"Easy," he called when he thought he was near enough to be heard. "It's me comin' in. The guy with the gun is dead."

Burt and Naomi stood up from behind a dead horse. The two schoolteachers came out of the coach where they had taken refuge. When he got near it became obvious to Longarm that the dead horses were already bloating and beginning to stink.

"All right, folks," he said, taking charge. "We got t' hike down to that relay station an' tell them what's happened to their southbound."

"Can't we just wait here for someone to come get us?" one of the teachers—he never had gotten their names right although one was Janice and the other Clarisse—piped up.

"Sure. If that's what you want t' do, feel free, but those

horses are already startin' to smell. By this time tomorrow their stink will gag a buzzard. Do what you want, though. Me, I'm walking. An' I'm doing it at night when it ain't so hot."

"How will you find your way?" the other one asked.

"The road is pretty obvious, ma'am. There's enough starlight for that, and the moon will be up soon," Longarm responded.

"What about the dead?" Burt asked.

"They'll bloat up an' stink, too, but they won't be any deader from the wait," Longarm said. "All right. Whoever is goin' with me . . . young lady, you're a prisoner so you got no choice; you walk along with me an' Burt whether you like it or not . . . whoever wants to walk, c'mon. We got miles to cover."

"These shoes are not made for walking," one of the teachers—perhaps it was Janice, perhaps it was Clarisse—said.

"If you got something better in your luggage, get it out an' put it on," Longarm said. "The rest of us will wait."

"Actually, I don't."

"Then walk in what you got or stay here until someone comes t' rescue you," Longarm told her.

"What about our luggage?" the other teacher asked.

"Whatever you like," Longarm said. "If you want t' carry it along, feel free. Otherwise leave it here t' be collected later on."

"Is it safe?"

Longarm broke out laughing. "Lady, just who d'you think is gonna steal it way the hell out here?"

"Oh, I . . . hadn't thought of that."

"Look, we're wasting time. Personally I'd like t' reach that relay station an' a hot cup o' coffee before the sun bakes us to crisps tomorrow," Longarm said.

Without further comment he motioned for Burt and the girl to follow and set off down the road leading south.

Chapter 32

Longarm's feet hurt like a son of a bitch. And his boots were low-heel boots that were designed for walking. He could just imagine what that middle-aged and probably far-out-of-shape schoolteachers' feet must feel like.

But they got there, damnit. They reached the relay station just before dawn and shook the station tender out of bed.

"I was wonderin' what happened to y'all," the man drawled. He introduced himself as Pete Vold and ushered everyone inside. "You must be beat. Set down there. I'll put on a pot of coffee an' then make you something to eat."

"How's about something to drink first thing," Longarm suggested. "We're all parched. Didn't have any water aboard and no one had a canteen with us."

"There's water in that pitcher there. It's clean. Cups on the shelf there," Vold said.

The relay station was basically one large room with a table and chairs to seat a dozen at a time. There were hooks screwed into the log wall close to the doorway and shelves

for the necessities of preparing meals. Vold had a lean-to
extending off the back for his reasonably private space. The
corrals and tack shed belonging to the Watson line were
arrayed off to one side of the station building.

"What happened to you?" Pete asked while he was busy
measuring out coffee grounds and building up the fire in
the stove.

Burt and Janice and Clarisse—at least on the long walk
Longarm had had a chance to figure out which of the schoolteachers was which—all tried to talk at once to explain their
ordeal. Pete oohed and ahhed at the appropriate points in
their narrative and probably ended up with a pretty good
understanding of what had happened.

"Do you have a telegraph here?" Longarm asked.

"Sorry. No." Pete closed the iron stove door with a clang
and wiped his hands on a towel. "I just send messages on
the daily up-and-down runs. That saves us the cost of putting in all those poles and buying wire." He grinned. "'Sides
which, I can't make out anything but noise when somebody
taps on a telegraph key." He set a pan on the stove and
started slicing bacon into it.

"I ran out of lard so's I can't make you biscuits this morning. There's supposed to be some coming on the next northbound," the busy station keeper said.

"Does the line even have a replacement coach?" Longarm
asked.

"Aye, we got a mud wagon, too. It's light. Two horses can
pull it. Since the big coach never got there yesterday I suppose they'll send the little one up this evening." He scratched
the beard stubble on his chin and said, "They'll have to
deliver any passengers on up to Thermopolis. That's a
requirement of the mail contract, I think. Probably take a
fresh team up with them as far as the stranded coach and
drive it back down this evening. Then tomorrow both the

southbounds can head back to Rawlins. Leastways that's how I would do it. Can one of you drive a four-up? I'd go myself but I have to stay here to tend the stock. What stock is left. You say the son of a bitch . . . sorry, ladies . . . you say this fella killed all four of our animals?"

"I'm afraid he did," Longarm said. "And say, you wouldn't have any cigars, would you? I smoked the last of mine on the way down here."

"No, sorry. I chew but I don't smoke," Vold said.

Each of the five stranded passengers filled up on water. Then bacon. Then coffee. Until Longarm's belly felt close to bursting, and he suspected the others were in the same condition.

"Pardon me now, folks, but I need to go out an' feed," Pete said when the guests had all been satisfied. By then the sun was fully up and the day was becoming hot. It would have been unbearable had they tried to make that hike in daytime.

"Can I help?" Longarm asked.

"Glad for the company," Pete said.

"Guard the prisoner, Burt. No, don't look at me like that. I know there's no place for her to run to, but it's our job to guard her anyway," Longarm told him.

He followed Pete Vold out to the set of corrals where the company livestock was rested between pulls and helped Vold throw hay.

"We have to have every scrap of our hay hauled in," Vold told him. "Same as the tour operators up at the hot springs. Can't cut so much as a stem around here."

"The way you have it laid out," Longarm said, "we'll be here overnight, then go south again tomorrow. Is that right?"

"Yes, sir, but I got blankets to accommodate emergency guests like this an' plenty of food. Well, except for the lard, that is. I hope they bring me some on the northbound like they're supposed to, but once that bacon grease cools I can use that this evening if I need to."

Pete dug his pitchfork into the side of a haystack beside the holding corral.

Chapter 33

The northbound coach—a well-used vehicle that once had been an army ambulance—arrived shortly after noon. Vold had beans, bacon, and coffee ready and fed everyone. There were two passengers on the northbound and several boxes of supplies for Pete Vold's relay station.

After lunch and a change of team, Pete and the driver, a man named Ed, tied four horses onto the back of the coach and Longarm climbed in.

They had to drive slowly to accommodate the spare horses tied in back, but they arrived at the disabled coach in mid-afternoon. Ed helped Longarm muscle the harness off the dead horses and onto the live ones, then without apology he climbed back onto the driving seat on his mud wagon and headed north to Thermopolis with his paying passengers aboard.

Longarm used the harnessed-but-as-yet-not-hitched team to drag the dead animals out of the road, then completely the hitch.

It had been a while since he had handled a four-horse hitch and it took a little while for him to become accustomed to it. He managed without causing any serious injury to the horses or to himself and arrived at the relay station just as the sun was sinking toward the horizon.

"I was beginnin' to wonder if you was all right," Pete said by way of greeting.

"I am now that I'm here in one piece," Longarm said, climbing down from the driving box.

He and Vold unhitched the team and turned them loose in the corral to rest overnight. The same horses would have to be put back in harness in the morning, so Vold fed them some grain as well as their usual hay. Longarm hoped the horses were not as tired as he was. After going the previous night awake and afoot and the day driving a stagecoach he was just about ready to keel over sideways.

"Wash up and come on in now," Pete said. "I have supper waiting."

"Pete," Longarm asked when he saw the spread of food on the long table, "d'you know how to cook anything other'n beans and bacon?"

"Ah, I got biscuits made this time now that Ed brought me a tub o' lard. And there's a surprise for after."

The surprise turned out to be a dried apple pie. Pete had soaked the apple pieces early in the afternoon and baked a more than presentable deep-dish pie with them.

"I take back all the mean things I said about you," Longarm told the man.

"What things?" Vold asked.

Longarm merely grinned in response.

That night Burt Hood spread his blanket close beside Naomi Foster's. Longarm was pleased to see that the youngster was taking his guard duties so seriously.

As for himself, he was not completely comfortable sleeping in the same room with a bunch of strangers. He took his blanket out beside the corrals, forked down a nice bed of hay, and placed his blanket on top of it.

The bed was soft, and the presence of the stars overhead and the soft sounds of the horses nearby were comforting. He closed his eyes and was asleep almost immediately.

Chapter 34

Longarm was sitting upright, .45 in hand, before he was consciously aware that he had been wakened.

He heard a yelp of surprise, blinked, realized it was the Wisconsin schoolteacher Janice Ruhl who had disturbed his sleep.

"Don't shoot, Marshal, it's just me," she bleated, obviously frightened by his reaction.

"Sorry." Longarm pushed the Colt back into its leather and set the revolver aside. He smiled. "I get touchy when I'm asleep. Keeps me alive, don't you see."

"Yes, of course, I . . . I had to get out of there," she stammered.

"Something wrong?" he asked.

"It's those young people. I can understand. In a way. But the sounds they are making are, um, distressful."

"What sorta sounds?"

"You know."

"Ma'am, if I knew I wouldn't ask."

"They are making love, Marshal. Oh, they are trying to

be quiet about it, but that is exactly what they are doing. Please don't say that I told you, though. That girl frightens me," Janice said. She sighed. "May I sit down? My legs are still worn-out from all that walking."

"Yes, of course." He patted the bed of soft hay beside him. "Sit here."

"I won't disturb you?"

"No, of course not," he lied. What he really wanted was to go back to sleep.

Janice settled close beside him and looked up at the brilliant stars overhead. "There is such beauty out here. This is the trip of a lifetime for me. For both of us, really. Back home we have to be jealous of our reputations. Here we can let our hair down and relax. Here no one is watching us and judging every little thing that we do."

"Is it really like that?" he asked.

"For a teacher it is, yes, even more than for most women, single or married."

"Have you never been married?"

"No, never. I will admit that I have taken lovers from time to time, but I've had to be careful about that, too. No one from close to home. Never anyone from our town." She sighed again. "This trip has been a wonderful adventure, but I have to admit to being disappointed that I couldn't find . . . couldn't find a man to keep me company." Janice laughed. "And I am afraid Clarisse is no substitute for that. May I ask you something, Marshal?"

"O' course. Anything," he said.

"Would you please kiss me?"

Chapter 35

Janice's lips were full and soft, and her tongue danced delicately with his. Her breath was sweet, carrying hints of mint. Which led him to suspect that she had had exactly this in mind even before she came out of the relay station.

He put an arm around her and gently lowered Janice to the blanket.

Her hands roved over his shoulders and his belly, silently giving him permission to do as much to her.

He deftly unbuttoned the bodice of her dress and slipped a hand inside. Her tit was large and soft, her nipple huge and dark. He bent his lips to her and gently sucked on her nipple. Janice responded by squirming under his touch and moaning, She cupped the back of his head in her hands and pulled him closer. He sucked harder and she cried out with pleasure.

Janice fumbled for the buttons at his fly, undid them, and reached inside. She gasped when she felt the size of him.

"Please. Do you mind?" If he had minded it would have already been too late. With an anxious cry, Janice pulled away from Longarm and bent to him, pressing the head of his cock to her cheek and breathing in the man smell of his pecker.

She peeled back his foreskin and ran her tongue over the throbbing head of his erection, then took him into the heat of her mouth, her fingers toying with his balls, one fingernail straying to his asshole while she continued to suck him.

Longarm allowed himself to come close to a climax, then gently pulled Janice off his dick and onto her back. He pushed her dress up, exposing pale thighs and a nest of dark, curly hair.

A touch proved that she was dripping wet with her own juices. Longarm slid a finger into her, and Janice stiffened and cried out.

"So long," she whispered. "It has been so very long since I felt a man's touch there."

"You're gonna feel a hell of a lot more'n just a finger," he assured her while he slid a knee between her legs to open her wider. Then, poised above her, he drove his cock into her.

Janice's flesh surrounded him. Her tits pillowed him. Her mouth and her tongue were wet and hot on his neck and throat, and she clutched at him with a strength he had not suspected.

She wrapped her legs around him, pressing him ever deeper, her gyrating hips urging him ever faster.

Longarm pumped his flesh into her hard and fast, and his sap rose quickly until it burst inside her body with a spasm of raw pleasure.

He shuddered, his dick quivering, and pounded her belly with his own.

Janice screamed and held him all the closer as she, too, reached a climax.

"So good," she whispered over and over again into his ear. "That was so very good."

He smiled and kissed her. "For me, too, lady."

When he started to withdraw, she stopped him. "Let me feel it inside me a little longer. Do you mind?"

Longarm chuckled. "That's not the sort o' thing a man minds, ma'am," he said and allowed his weight to settle onto her, marveling anew how even the smallest women—which Janice Ruhl was not—can take a man's weight on top of them with no apparent discomfort.

He lay his head down against her and closed his eyes. He must have dozed a little because the next time he paid attention a sliver of moon had come up, and the constellations were in a much different position.

If Janice minded, she did not show it. His cock was still inside her and Longarm began to grow hard again, his dick stiffening and filling her anew.

Janice smiled and began to rock her hips slowly up and down.

Chapter 36

Longarm walked Janice back to the relay station and went inside to check on Burt Hood and their prisoner. Hood was awake, sitting silently beside the sleeping girl. He got up when Longarm entered and came over to greet him.

"I'm keeping watch," he said, "but I'm getting awfully sleepy."

"It's all right for you to sleep. Just stay close an' try to wake up if she moves around. She ain't going anywhere by herself anyway, not out this far from civilization. An' you need some sleep if you're gonna be any good to me," Longarm said. "By the way, I, um, I heard you an' her might've been making some noises together."

"Truth is, we were talking. We got to giggling about some things," Burt said.

"You weren't fucking the lady?" Longarm asked bluntly.

"No, of course not. It wouldn't be proper to have relations with someone in your custody, would it," Burt said.

"I'm glad you recognize that fact," Longarm told him. But he thought Burt seemed a little nervous when he was denying the contact. "Keep your hands to yourself an' your britches buttoned. We'll have her to Denver in a few more days, an' we'll be shut of her. Until then be careful what you do."

"It was that schoolteacher who told you we were fooling around, wasn't it?" Burt said.

"Doesn't matter who said it. What matters is that you don't do it. Remember, everything you do now reflects on Billy Vail an' on the marshals' service. A man has t' be a mite careful with what he does," Longarm said.

"I won't forget that," Burt said solemnly.

"Go on back to bed now an' get some sleep. We got another long day tomorrow."

"Yes, sir."

Longarm glanced across the big room to where Janice Ruhl was lying down next to her friend Clarisse. She acted like she was already asleep, and perhaps she really was. Or perhaps she did not want anyone to suspect what she had been up to out by the haystacks. Either way was fine by him. He certainly did not want to tarnish the lusty lady's reputation.

He helped himself to a cup of cold coffee and went back out to his rather rumpled bedding, feeling much more relaxed than he had been earlier that evening.

Chapter 37

"Whoa. Whoa, you sorry son of a bitch!" Longarm brought the stocky bay horse back down onto its feet with a yank on the lead rope and backed it into place as the near wheeler. Burt hooked it into the traces, and Longarm went to bring out the off wheeler.

Neither Longarm nor Burt Hood was familiar with either the horses or the process. The station keeper was busy feeding and watering the other horses and assumed Longarm could handle the four heavy horses. That would perhaps have been easier if the horses had cooperated. As it was they apparently resented having to work two days in a row. The animals were accustomed to having a day of rest between their days of work.

Still, between them Longarm and Hood managed to get the team harnessed and hooked in place. Longarm climbed onto the driving box while Burt went inside to get the women.

"We'll be passing some ranches further south, an' the

next relay station is fairly close to folks," Longarm advised Burt, "so's you'd best put handcuffs on the prisoner."

Burt looked up at him from the ground. "Can't we ask for her promise not to attempt an escape?" he asked. "I'm sure she would give her word about it."

"Sonny, she gave her word to that postmaster over to Buffalo, too. see how much good that did," Longarm said sternly. "She wears the bracelets an' that's that."

"Yes, sir." Reluctantly Burt caught the set of handcuffs that Longarm tossed down to him and put them on Naomi Foster.

When his passengers were inside the stagecoach, Longarm released the brake and took up contact with the bits of the four-up. "Hyah. Hyah there."

The big horses moved into an easy trot, the coach starting with a lurch, then swaying and bouncing on the leather springs.

"Whoa. Whoa, you sons of bitches." Longarm hauled back on the driving lines and brought the coach to a stop outside the Watson Express Line headquarters. It had been a long day of dust and heat. His forearms ached from the unaccustomed effort of handling the driving lines, and his throat was dry. He wanted a drink and a cigar—in that order—and he was damned sure looking forward to climbing down off the stagecoach.

"Who the hell are you and what are you doing with my coach?" the stage line managed demanded, peering up at Longarm with suspicion.

"Let me get down off o' here an' I'll explain," Longarm said.

"It better be good or I'll have the law on you," the manager threatened.

"Mister, I *am* the law, so hush yourself an' listen." He set the brake and wrapped the lines around the whip socket, then dismounted while the passengers got out.

"And why is that luggage on the roof? Is the boot all that full?" the manager demanded.

"Is that a cigar I see in your pocket, man?" Without waiting for an invitation, Longarm plucked the stogie out of the manager's pocket and stuck it between his teeth.

"Hey! Quit that."

"Yeah. Sorry." Longarm bit the twist off the end of the cigar, struck a match and built a bright coal. He drew in a long puff of smoke, exhaled with a smile and said, "All right. We can go inside now an' I'll tell you what's been going on. Burt, bring the prisoner. An' you, mister, you can have the luggage brought down t' where folks can get to it. You, uh, wouldn't happen t' have a bottle o' rye in there, would you? No? Burt, give me the prisoner. You go to that saloon over there an' fetch us a bottle, would you, please." He gave Naomi a hard look and said, "Be good or I'll cuff you behind your back. I doubt you'd like that. Come inside, mister. There's a lot you got t' catch up on."

Chapter 38

"The next eastbound passenger is in the middle o' the damn night," Longarm said as they were exiting the Watson office, "an' I'm not in any mood for another night on the road. We'll get rooms an' head back to Denver tomorrow. Unless you got some objection."

"I have one," Naomi Foster grumbled.

"I wasn't askin' you," he replied. "Burt?"

"No, it's all right with me."

"That's settled then. You an' the prisoner wait here. I'll go see what I can find in the way of rooms."

Half an hour later Longarm came back to collect them. "I found the perfect deal," he said, smiling.

The perfect deal turned out to be one ordinary hotel room plus a servant's room that had one door and no window.

"You and me will share the room," Longarm said. "We'll take turns sleeping. The girl can have the little room downstairs while the one of us on guard duty will sit outside her door. That way she can have some privacy t' do whatever it is that women need an' she won't have t' be in chains while she does it. Should be ideal."

Burt nodded and looked at Naomi, who was pretending to ignore the conversation. But she looked down at her handcuffs and her lips thinned a little in a hidden smile.

"Come along then." Longarm led them to the Antrose Hotel.

"I'll take the first watch," Burt volunteered. "You must be awful tired after handling those horses all day. I was able to rest in the stagecoach this afternoon."

"I am more than a little wore out," Longarm admitted. "I could use a little sleep." He carried their gear upstairs to the room he and Burt would take turns sharing while Burt put Naomi in her small, isolated room off the hotel kitchen and set a chair in front of the door.

"Mighty convenient for grabbing a bite o' supper," Longarm said when he came back down to check on Burt and the prisoner. "Me, I'm gonna grab a chicken leg an' a chunk o' bread and carry them up to the room with me. I'll be down around midnight to relieve you. I've already asked the hotel t' give the both of you something to eat."

"Sounds fine with me," Burt said. "You go on and get some sleep. You look like you need it."

"What about me?" Naomi asked. "Can I get these bracelets off of me, you son of a bitch?"

Longarm looked at Burt and smiled. "I love it when she talks dirty."

"I don't have the handcuff key," Burt reminded him.

Longarm nodded and dug the key out of his vest pocket. He handed it over to Burt, who unfastened the handcuffs and ushered the girl into her room. Burt closed the door and set his chair in front of it. "I'll be fine down here. Go on now. Get some sleep."

Six hours later Longarm woke up, quickly washed and

dressed, and went back downstairs to the hotel kitchen. The chair in front of Naomi's room was empty.

Inside the room he found Burt lying on the floor, his trousers around his ankles.

And no sign of Naomi Foster.

Chapter 39

"Wake up, you son of a bitch." Longarm kicked Burt in his naked butt. When that did no good he got a glass of water from the bedside pitcher and poured it on Burt's head.

That worked.

"I . . . I . . ."

"Oh, I know what you did," Longarm growled. "You decided to get a piece of ass. *From a prisoner in your custody!* What the hell were you thinking? No, don't answer that. You weren't thinking. Your dick was. Of all the stupid . . ."

"I didn't mean for this to happen," Burt said with a groan and a shake of his head. "I'll tell you the truth, Longarm. That girl, she gives the best blow job in the whole world. She came on to me up in Thermopolis. Said she just loved to suck cock and would I mind. Well, let me tell you. It was something special. She can take a man's dick all the way down into her throat. Clean past the mouth and into the throat, I'm telling you. I never felt anything like it."

"Jesus, kid, lots of women can do that. So what happened here?" Longarm asked.

"I was sitting in my chair, right beside the door where you told me to stay, and Naomi whispered to me through the door. She said she wanted . . . she wanted more of me. Said she wanted to drink my come. I got . . . I just couldn't stand thinking about that. So I whispered back would she give me her parole and promise not to run if I came inside. She said she promised. So I went in and lay down and she pulled my britches down and started in on me, and the next thing I knew I . . . it's more like I heard a thump on my head. Here, I think."

Burt reached up and rather gingerly touched the left side of his head. He winced when his fingers encountered something there.

"Sit up," Longarm said. "Let me take a look." He helped Burt off the floor and onto the side of the cot and felt of the spot Burt indicated. "You got a lump that would do a mama goose proud."

"I just wish the bitch had killed me," Burt said.

"It's a thought," Longarm agreed. "At least you've finally figured out that a deputy's got no business fucking a prisoner. Hell, kid, that's why they sent two of us up here, so's the bitch couldn't claim she was raped an' maybe get off. An' keep in mind, kid, if she wasn't a bitch you wouldn't be having her in handcuffs."

Longarm stood back and sighed. "Reckon now we got t' go an' catch her again. But this time the only time I want t' see you unbutton your pants is when you got t' take a shit. D'you understand me? Understand me clear?" Longarm shook his head and scowled.

"Yes, sir," Burt said meekly. Then he felt of his waist and yelped.

"Now what?" Longarm said with a grunt.

"My pistol. It's gone. I guess . . . she must have taken it."

"Lordy, boy, you only got one talent, an' it's for letting your guns be stole off o' you. All right. Let's go see can we borry one off the local law here an' then see what we can figure out about that scurrilous bitch an' how to get her back again."

Chapter 40

Longarm pounded on the door of the town marshal's office until a bleary-eyed deputy finally woke up and came to see what the problem might be.

"Sorry t' roust you out," Longarm said, "but I'm a deputy United States marshal an' I need the loan of one o' your shotguns."

"You're who?" the scrawny deputy asked, rubbing first his eyes and then the dark stubble on his chin.

"Deputy U.S. marshal," Longarm repeated, "an' I need your help." He pulled out his wallet to display the badge that was pinned inside.

"A shotgun, you say?" the deputy mumbled.

"Or a six-gun. Whatever you got."

The young deputy yawned, shuddered, pushed the door open wide. "Come inside. I'll see what I can find. You're sure you . . . never mind. I don't want to let just any of the town's guns go, but we might have something in the drunk closet."

"Drunk closet?" Burt asked.

The deputy grinned. "When we haul in drunks on Saturday nights. Or any other nights for that matter. Anyway, if they're waving guns around we take them off o' the fellows and stick them in this closet back here. In the morning sometimes they remember to collect their guns and sometimes they don't. And sometimes they have to run catch a train and don't have time to think about such things. They just leave it behind. So let me look and see if we have anything in there." Over his shoulder he added, "Every three months or so the town auctions off any confiscated stuff like that. It brings in a pretty penny, let me tell you."

The "closet" he referred to was actually more like a small room. It held an odd assortment of saddles and bags and even something that looked suspiciously like a wooden leg. Of interest to Longarm was a single-barrel shotgun with an exceptionally long barrel and beavertail forearm. It was the only gun in the room.

"Does that thing shoot?" he asked the deputy.

The man shrugged. "Damn if I know. I recall that the fellow who owned it was on his way to Salt Lake City. Said he wanted to hunt ducks. It's only a sixteen, though."

"Any shells for it?" Longarm asked. He turned to Burt and asked, "I know you can't shoot worth shit with a pistol. How are you with a scattergun?"

Burt grinned. "Marshal, I grew up hunting on the Chesapeake. Tell me what feathers you want shot off a bird, and I can do it, wing, tail, or the other wing."

"Even with a sixteen gauge?" Longarm asked.

"Even with a four-ten, marshal. I don't want to brag but . . . I can do it."

To the Rawlins deputy Longarm said, "We'll take it. And the shells?"

The deputy shook his head. "Sorry."

Burt broke the action and peered down the barrel. "At

least somebody took good care of it. The action feels tight, and the barrel is clean." His grin flashed again. "Maybe I can hang onto this one, huh?"

"Yeah, if only because that thing is so ugly no one would want t' steal it." He asked the deputy, "Where can we find some shells for this thing?"

"No place at this time of night. In the morning, any hardware or gun store, of course."

"That will have to do then," Longarm said. "Thanks for your help. We'll bring your gun back when we can."

"Don't bother. We got no use for it," the deputy said.

Both Longarm and Burt thanked the man again, and Burt carried the ungainly shotgun in the crook of his arm when they stepped out into the chill night air.

"Now where?" Burt asked.

"Now we find a saloon that's open at this hour."

"Aren't we going to go after Naomi?"

Longarm gave him a hard look. "Just exactly where would you look for her?"

"I, uh, I guess I don't know," Burt said.

"Which is exactly why you and me are going to go have a drink an' think about where she might run to an' how she intends t' get there."

"Oh, I see," Burt said meekly and followed Longarm toward the nearest saloon and gaming house.

Chapter 41

"The bitch doesn't have any money on her. We know that for a fact because we searched her," Longarm said over a glass of passable—but not Jespers rye whiskey. "She'll find it hard to travel without money. Can't take a train, I wouldn't think, although she might be able to trade a fuck or a blow job for a ride on a ranch wagon."

"How much did she steal from that post office in Buffalo?" Burt asked.

"Y'know, I never heard an exact amount," Longarm said, "but it must have been considerable to justify taking it."

"Yet she didn't have any money on her when that town marshal up in Thermopolis arrested her. Which means she probably has it stashed somewhere up there. And that means she will most likely go there and try to recover it." Burt smiled, obviously pleased with himself for coming up with that deduction.

Longarm was pleased with him, too. "Good thinking, kid. Assuming that you're right, that narrows down our search considerable. We know where she's likely to go. Don't know how she intends t' get there, of course."

"The stagecoach?" Burt suggested.

"Maybe, but she still has the problem of not having any money."

Burt took a drink and frowned. "This just isn't as good as what I'm used to," he said.

"Have a couple more drinks an' it will all taste just fine," Longarm said, laughing.

Burt had another drink.

Longarm got up and walked over to the bar. He bought some cigars—they did not have any cheroots, but they did stock some nice panatelas with a pale wrapper leaf—and another pair of drinks.

"She knows we'll be looking for her," Longarm said when he got back to the table. "I'm betting she'll hole up someplace an' try to wait us out before she runs north again. She needs a place t' stay, and she needs money. She might possibly be able to get some money tonight by rolling a drunk for his poke or by offering to fuck for pay. I wouldn't put that past the little bitch. But which? An' where?"

"This is all my fault," Burt moaned over his third glass of rye.

"Yes, it is," Longarm agreed.

"I'm sorry, Longarm."

"Sorry don't feed the dog, kid."

"So what do we do now?" Burt asked.

Longarm drained his rye and put the empty glass down onto the table. "Now we assume that she's got hold of some money somehow an' can travel again. So now you are gonna help me look for her in every saloon in the town an' be watching when every train makes a stop at the Rawlins depot. We want t' make sure she don't sneak aboard although I don't think she would. That is, I don't think there is anything east or west of here that she'll be interested in. I'm thinking she wants to get back up north to the money she's got stashed up there. But we want t' be thorough so we'll watch the trains. Then come morning when the northbound coach leaves, we'll be watching that, too. Meantime we check the saloons an' we check the hotels an' we prowl the streets and the alleys, an' we keep on doing it until we find the bitch."

"This is all my fault," Burt again moaned. "I just wish . . ."

"Wishing don't change shit, kid. What's done is done. Now we get about setting it right again. Finish your drink. We got work t' do."

Longarm lighted a cigar while Burt polished off his glass of rye. Then they stood and headed out to look for Naomi Foster.

Chapter 42

"Kid, I'm gonna post you on the railroad platform here. Keep watch even between train arrivals. You never know when or where she might show up, but be especially careful when there's a train stopped here. I doubt she would know how to ride the rods underneath the railcars, but I wouldn't count on that, so look for her."

"Where will you be?" Burt asked.

Longarm motioned toward the town where most of the homes and businesses were dark. "I'm gonna make the rounds of all the saloons an' the hotels. Damn woman has to be someplace, and one way or another we are gonna catch her again. But this time she won't be giving any blow jobs. You understand me, boy? This time she stays in 'cuffs. And your britches stay buttoned."

"Yes, sir," Burt mumbled. "It's my fault that she got away. I understand." His expression brightened and he managed a wan smile. "But that girl sure does give a great blow job. The best I ever had, and that is for certain sure."

"A damned expensive one," Longarm said. "And I'm not talkin' about money."

Burt took up position on the railroad depot's platform, and Longarm turned back toward town. He intended to start at one end of Rawlins and work his way toward the other. Saloons, hotels, and anything else that was open at this middle-of-the-night hour.

He was perhaps a third of the way through when a muzzle flash blossomed out of the mouth of an alley across the street from him and a bullet shattered a glass window beside him.

Longarm hit the ground, Colt .45 in hand, eyes searching that alley but without result.

"Fuck it," he muttered, leaping to his feet and charging for the alley, zigzagging back and forth as he ran so as to throw off the other person's aim.

Chapter 43

Longarm stopped and pressed his back against the wall of Hatton's Menswear. He took a deep breath and stepped around the corner into the alley mouth, Colt held at the ready.

He saw nothing, heard nothing. Half a heartbeat later he heard running footsteps and a dark figure was silhouetted against the paler light at the far end of the alley.

Longarm snapped a shot at the dark figure just as it turned the corner behind Hatton's, knew he had missed, and cursed under his breath.

He was sure, though, that the figure he so briefly glimpsed was that of a man. It had not been Naomi Foster who shot at him. Instead it was a male, although why any man in Rawlins would want Custis Long dead he did not know. There seemed no logical reason for the ambush.

While he was busy trying to think things through, Longarm's hands were working on their own tasks, almost automatically punching out the spent cartridge case and replacing it. He generally carried his revolver with only five chambers loaded so the hammer could safely rest on an empty chamber. Now he dropped a sixth cartridge into the normally empty position, then snapped the loading gate closed.

He waited for his eyes to adjust to the deep darkness of the alley—it was not impossible that there could be a pair of would-be assassins involved, one showing himself to draw their quarry into the alley and a second to shoot him when he stepped into their trap—and very carefully advanced through the alley toward the back of the store.

There was no second assassin, but it was not the sort of thing a man wanted to take for granted. After all, it was a matter he could be wrong about only once.

Behind Hatton's he saw . . . nothing. The shooter had as good as disappeared.

He did see lights in the next block, light coming from the back of a saloon he had already visited in his search for Naomi Foster. It was the only logical place where the shooter might have gone.

Longarm picked up his pace and hurried across the side street to the back of the saloon.

As he had expected, there was a back door that led to an outhouse where patrons of the saloon could get rid of some of the beer they had consumed.

Longarm pulled the door open and stepped inside.

"Hello again, Marshal," the barman said, nodding. "Still no sign of that girl you were looking for."

Colt still in hand and his eyes flicking back and forth to assess the crowd, Longarm stepped to the bar.

"Right now I'm looking for the man that came in through this back door a minute ago," Longarm said.

"Right over there," the bartender said, motioning toward a group of men gathered around a card table.

"Which . . . ?"

"He's the fellow in the leather jacket," the helpful barman said. "On the left."

Longarm grunted his thanks, eyes locked on the man who had shot at him for no reason. Except, he realized, there had been a reason. There must have been. A man does not try to kill another for no reason at all. It was just that Longarm did not know what this fellow's reason had been.

It was something he truly did want to discover. After all, there had been several such incidents recently. It would be quite all right with him if this shit were to stop.

Colt in hand, Longarm approached the swarthy, dark-bearded man in the leather jacket.

Chapter 44

Longarm walked to the front door of the place but veered aside before he got there and circled around the room until he could come up behind the man in the leather jacket.

Moving silently on the sawdust-covered floor, he closed in behind the shooter, shoved his Colt back into the leather, then reached down and lifted the man's revolver from its holster.

"Hey!" The man yelped loudly, jumped out of his chair and spun around toward Longarm.

"You're under arrest, damn you," Longarm barked just as loudly.

His Smith & Wesson .44 gone, the man could be reasonably expected to give up. He apparently did not know that. Instead of submitting to arrest he lunged forward, throwing himself at Longarm and sending Longarm backward with Leather Jacket on top of him.

The two of them struggled for only a moment before they toppled onto the floor.

Longarm grappled with the man, who was heavier built

if a few inches shorter in height. Whoever he was, and why
ever he wanted to kill Longarm, the man was strong as a
young bull and twice as quick.

The two of them rolled in the sawdust, knocked over a
cuspidor, and rolled again, coming to a stop with Leather
Jacket on top.

Longarm was hampered by having Leather Jacket's
revolver in one hand. He elbowed the man in the ribs and
used his free hand to pummel his face repeatedly.

Leather Jacket threw himself backward to gain some
separation between Longarm and himself. Then from
beneath that leather jacket he pulled a knife.

"Aw, shit," Longarm growled.

Without pausing to think, he thumbed back the hammer
on the Smith & Wesson .44-40 and pulled the trigger at
point-blank range.

The bullet entered just beneath Leather Jacket's rib cage
and traveled at an upward angle, presumably passing through
the man's heart on its way. The muzzle blast scorched his
shirt and set it on fire, but the flame quickly died away.

Leather Jacket turned pale and collapsed on top of Longarm, his knife trapped between them but cutting neither man.

He tried to speak but produced only a red bubble as blood
poured into his lungs.

Longarm pushed him off, rolled, and came to his knees.

"Don't die, damn you. Don't you dare die before I can
ask you some questions."

The entreaty went unheeded. Within a minute Leather
Jacket's eyes rolled back in his head, the light of life having
gone out of them, and the man went limp.

The men he had been playing cards with were standing,
spectators to the life-and-death struggle that had just
unfolded in front of them.

Longarm dropped the dead man's revolver on the card table and produced his wallet and badge. "Hold on here, you fellas. I got some questions for you about your friend here."

Chapter 45

"Marshal, we three live here. We work second shift over at the rail yard and come in pretty much every night after we clock out. We've known each other for years, but we never saw that fellow before he came in and joined the game." Tyler Branscom reached for his drink and took a swallow, then continued.

"We play a low-stakes game and it doesn't bother us if some stranger takes any money off the table." His smile flashed. "Doesn't bother us if some stranger wants to *leave* money on the table, either."

"What about this man?" Longarm asked.

Branscom shook his head. "We really don't know anything. He just sat in not five minutes before you got here."

"He had a Spanish accent," Boyd Parker put in.

"He didn't say anything about where he was from or what he was doing here?" Longarm asked.

All three of the local men shook their heads. "No, sir, not a word," Jens Swanson said. "He took a handful of coins out of his pocket and put it on the table. Come to think of it, what do we do with his money? Not that there's so awful much of it, maybe two or three dollars total, but it doesn't belong to us."

"I'd say you should give it to whoever 'tis here that handles buryings and such," Longarm said. "That and whatever else he might have on him. Any idea did he get here by train? Stagecoach? Whatever?"

"No idea how he got here or where he might have been staying," Tyler Branscom said.

"But he had a Spanish accent, you say," Longarm said.

The three men who had been playing cards with the dead man nodded. "He had some English but not much," Branscom said, "and none of us speaks Spanish."

Longarm knelt and went through the pockets of the dead man, but he had no identifying papers on him to suggest who he was or why he tried to kill Longarm.

He shoved the Smith & Wesson back into the dead man's holster. Taking it for Burt Hood would have been the same as stealing the gun's value from the local undertaker. Unless the dead had relatives to pay for their burial, the custom was that their possessions should go to pay for the costs of planting them.

Besides, Longarm thought, Burt would just lose the damn thing if he passed it along to the young deputy. Deputy-in-training was more like it. And the boy had a hell of a long way to go.

"If you think of anything that might tell me where he was from or at least where he was staying here in town, look me up an' let me know, please, fellas," Longarm said.

"We will, Marshal."

"We surely will."

"You can count on it, Marshal."

Longarm rubbed his jaw and smoothed his mustache. "All right then. Thank you for your help."

Spanish, he thought as he left the saloon. Presumably Mexican. That fit a pattern. But why? That was the main question. *Why?*

When he made the rounds of the hotels in town he would have to ask about this dead Mexican as well as look for Naomi Foster.

Chapter 46

Longarm found the Mexican's hotel in the wee hours of the morning. He had been staying in a fifty-cent flop called the Alameda.

"The man owes us money, Marshal," the Alameda's manager whined.

"I'm not trying to take his stuff," Longarm said, "but I need t' look it over."

"How do I know you won't be taking the man's valuables for yourself?" the manager complained. The man reminded Longarm of a weasel in both appearance and demeanor. He had a weak chin and rheumy eyes, and Longarm wanted to reach across the counter and smack him one.

Longarm reached across the counter and took the man by the front of his shirt instead, pulling him forward until the two were nose to nose. "Because if you give me any shit I'm gonna have this rat hole declared a crime scene an' shut it down for three, four days or so. Could be longer. You know how slow some folks can work." Longarm smiled, the expression hard and cold and with no hint of mirth in it. "Or you could give me the key now an' take me up to whatever room the fellow was in. Your choice, mister."

"If you will turn me loose, Marshal, I'll get that key for you," the manager said.

"Thank you." Longarm released his grip on the man's shirtfront. Two minutes later he was inside room number three on the second floor of the seedy little trackside hotel.

The Mexican had signed the hotel register with an X. Not that there was anything unusual about that. The law required that a register be kept but on the two pages Longarm saw there was only one signature. Everyone else simply marked an X. Longarm had been hoping that the dead man would at least have left his name behind. He had not.

Inside the airless, poorly furnished room the man had left only a cloth sack that contained two shirts—clean—one pair of socks—soiled—and three loose pistol cartridges.

Under the thin pad that passed for a pillow Longarm found a printed flyer of some sort, written in Spanish. The only words on it that he could understand were DEP MAR CUSTIS LONG. That captured his attention. He folded the flyer and stuck it in his pocket to be translated later.

There still was no sign of Naomi Foster, though.

Longarm walked over to the railroad platform, only a few steps away, and brought Burt up on his progress. Or lack of it.

"Say, you don't happen t' speak Spanish, do you?" he asked, thinking about that flyer.

"No, not me. Why?"

Longarm explained.

"Can I see it?"

"Hell, why not." Longarm brought the flyer out and unfolded it for Burt, which satisfied the young man's curiosity but did nothing to explain the purpose of the flyer. Burt shrugged and handed the flyer back to Longarm, who once again folded the sheet and tucked it away.

"Now what?" Burt asked.

"Now you keep watch here whilst I finish checking the hotels an' saloons for that girl," Longarm said.

"When are we going to sleep?" Burt asked.

Longarm feigned an expression of shock. "Sleep!" he cried. "Sleep? Kid, you don't sleep. You're tough. You're a deputy. Forget sleep. You can sleep next winter maybe. If you get some time off, that is."

Burt looked like he believed him.

Longarm grinned and clapped the young man on the shoulder. "Keep on doin' what you're doin' here. I got to finish up looking for that girl. The bitch has t' be someplace, and we're gonna find her. Mark my words. We are gonna find her."

"Yes, sir." Burt sounded like he did not believe that himself, but he dutifully said it. "We'll find her for sure."

Chapter 17

Longarm returned to the platform shortly after dawn to find Burt dozing on one of the benches. At least he did wake up and sit up straighter at the sound of Longarm's approach. He had dropped the long-barreled shotgun sometime during the night. He hastily picked it up now.

"Anything?" Burt asked.

Longarm shook his head. "Not a damn thing. Let's go get some breakfast."

They walked to a nearby café and sat where they could look out the window and keep an eye on the railroad platform. There was no train scheduled for another two hours, but that did not mean Naomi could not show up.

"By now," Longarm said, "she might have money t' spend. She has your pistol so she could've robbed someone. Which reminds me, we need to go check with the town marshal an' see if anybody has reported being robbed by someone matching her description. Or she could've given somebody a fuck or a blow job t' get some money. No way to check on that without interviewing every son of a bitch in Rawlins. Or she might . . . shit, I dunno. She's a slippery one."

Longarm scowled. "Money. That's the key to finding Naomi. Now that I think about it, the woman is stone-cold broke. Doesn't have a penny on her. We searched her. Would've found it if she had anything on her. But she's wanted for robbing some from the post office over in Buffalo, and that must've been a big haul or it wouldn't have been worth the taking. Not from a government outfit like the United States post office. That is some serious shit right there. I never got the details, but she has to 've taken a bunch."

He reached for his coffee cup and sipped at it, his eyes gazing off into some unseen distance while he thought.

Then he sat up straighter and smiled. "An' that tells us where she's headed now," he said.

"It does?" Burt looked thoroughly mystified by Longarm's sudden change of demeanor from pensive to pleased. "How does the woman being broke tell us anything?"

"We know she must have took a large amount out of that post office, kid, an' we know she didn't have it on her when she was captured up in Thermopolis. So she's got it stashed someplace up there. So that's where she'll be headed now. She'll be going back north t' get to her stolen money. She might lay low for a while. But that's where she'll be going sooner or later. Guar-own-tee!"

"So we're going back to Thermopolis?" Burt asked.

"Aye, we are. We got a few things t' do first, but that's where we're headed. On the stagecoach if the northbound is scheduled for today or we'll rent horses if need be, but we're headed north today, boy."

Burt looked pleased. He began shoveling eggs and fried potatoes in as fast as he could handle them or a little bit quicker.

Chapter 48

"No, there's no northbound stage today," Longarm said as he emerged from the Watson Express office. Burt had been left on the street to keep watch in case Naomi showed herself. "Did you see anything?"

Burt shook his head. "Nothing except a couple dogs screwing."

"Not what we're hoping for," Longarm said.

"So from here we go over to the livery to rent some horses?" Burt asked.

"Not quite yet. First we find a blacksmith. Or a gun shop where they do repairs."

"I saw one of them two blocks over," Burt said. "What do we want them for?"

"For that smoke pole you're carrying," Longarm said, motioning toward the Long Tom sixteen-gauge duck gun that Burt had.

Burt raised an eyebrow but dutifully led the way several blocks down and one over to a sign that read GEO. SANDS, GUNSMITH.

Inside the shop they found a barrel-chested black man with gray hair and beard.

"Are you George Sands?" Longarm asked.

"I am." The man's voice was a rich baritone that rumbled out of his belly like approaching thunder.

Longarm took Burt's duck gun and laid it on the counter. "We need some work done on this thing if you can do it while we wait."

"All right. I can give you the time. Remains to be seen if I can do what you want. So what is it that you need done to this cheap piece of trash?"

"We need the barrel cut down to just ahead of the hand guard and the stock cut off to make it like a pistol grip. Then we need a band put around what's left of the barrel and an eyelet on what's left of the butt and a sling between those, a long sling so the gun will carry about waist high when the sling is draped over the shoulder," Longarm said.

Sands smiled. "I see what it is that you want, mister. Just one thing. I'm not abetting any banditry, am I? I wouldn't do such a thing, not for any amount of money."

Longarm showed his badge and introduced himself.

"That's all right then," Sands said. "Come back in an hour. That will be plenty of time for me to do what you want. But for a rush job like that, um, two dollars?"

The way he said it suggested he could have been bargained down on the price, probably as low as half of what he was asking, but Longarm said, "That sounds fair, Mr. Sands. We'll be back in an hour." To Burt he said, "Come on, kid. Let's go find some horses t' rent."

Chapter 49

Longarm drew rein in front of the gunsmith's shop and dismounted, Burt Hood beside him.

Inside, George Sands held up a much improved and in fact quite handsome sixteen-gauge handgun. It had a leather strap with buckles to adjust the way it hung off the shoulder, and he had wrapped the handgrip with thin leather as well.

"Now that is a handsome job," Longarm said admiringly. "Thank you."

"My pleasure, sir."

Longarm handed the shortened shotgun to Burt and said to Sands, "My only problem is that this job is worth a lot more than two dollars. I wouldn't feel right about paying so little for such a good job." He dug into his pocket and found a five-dollar half eagle, which he gave to the gunsmith. "We'll need to buy a box of shells, too. The heaviest you have in sixteen gauge."

"That would be number two," Sands said, turning to his shelves. "Included in the price, let's say."

Burt slipped the leather keeper over his shoulder and

smiled at the way the modified shotgun hung. He picked up the box of shells, loaded the shotgun, and dropped a handful of the shells into his coat pocket.

Before they left the shop Burt removed his coat, hung the shotgun over his shoulder, and put the coat back on. "Perfect," he said.

"Okay, kid. Let's go find us a felon," Longarm said, heading out to the horses.

Just past noon they passed the southbound stagecoach. The driver pulled up to chat with them. And to take the opportunity to roll himself a cigarette.

Longarm recalled how hard driving a four-up was on the wrists and certainly did not begrudge the man his break.

"We're looking for a young woman," Longarm announced. "A Miss Naomi Foster. My partner here will tell you what she looks like." He grinned and added, "He knows her better'n I do."

Burt shot a dirty look in Longarm's direction, then described Naomi for the jehu.

The driver dug a fingernail into his beard, then said, "I saw such a woman, but I'm pretty sure her name was different. A Miss Susan Olson, she said she was, but she looked like you say, even dressed the same."

"That would be her, friend. Where'd you happen t' see her?"

"Up at the relay station. Her and a wagon of goods of some sort. I never asked what they were hauling, but they were headed north."

"When was that, mister?" Longarm asked.

"That was maybe an hour back, maybe a little more."

Longarm glanced at Burt, then nodded. "Could be our girl. Must be. Thank you, friend." He touched the brim of his Stetson to the driver and again to the passengers inside the coach as he and Burt rode past the heavy coach.

Once clear of the coach, where they would not be kicking up dust on the passengers, Longarm gigged his rented buckskin into a ground-eating lope.

Chapter 50

"That could be them," Longarm said as a train of three wagons came into view on the road ahead. They already passed the spot where the southbound coach had been waylaid days earlier. The spot was marked by the presence of four vultures off to the side where the would-be assassin lay dead and rotting.

Once they had the wagons in sight it took Longarm and Burt the better part of an hour to catch up with them. As they closed on the little caravan Longarm looked for Naomi. She had to be riding in one of the wagons, but he could not see her.

"Whoa up there, mister," Longarm called as they came abreast of the lead wagon. "I'm an officer of the law, an' I got official business with you."

The wagon master was a young man with a red beard and gray eyes. He had a bullwhip on the wagon seat beside him but did not appear to be armed.

"Show a badge, mister, to prove you're who you say you are," he challenged.

Longarm nodded and pulled out his wallet, flipped it open to display the badge as requested. "Satisfied?"

"Yes, so I am." The man held a hand up to signal the wagons behind his and pulled back on his driving lines. "Whoa, boys. Whoa now."

"We're looking for a woman name of Naomi Foster. Could be calling herself Susan Olson now," Longarm said.

"You want to talk with Susan?" The driver stood and turned to look back to the other wagons. "She's . . . well, hell, she was right back there a little while ago." He raised his voice and shouted, "Thomas. Where'd the lady go?"

"She wanted to get out of the sun, George. I told her she could crawl under the tarpaulin," Thomas called back to him.

Longarm wheeled his buckskin back toward that second wagon. "Sorry to hold you up here, mister, but that woman is wanted on federal charges. I'm going to have to take her into custody."

"Oh, shit, mister, I didn't know," Thomas blurted.

"It's all right, friend. You aren't in no trouble," Longarm told him. "Fact is, we got no way to carry her ourselves. We'll have t' ask you to carry her on to Thermopolis with you till we can catch a southbound stagecoach out o' there."

Longarm rode up close beside the halted wagon and called, "You almost made it, Naomi, but not quite. Come out from under that tarp so's I can put your bracelets back on. We'll take care o' you from here."

A small hand peeled the tarpaulin back, and Naomi stood up, blinking in the sunshine.

Longarm motioned Burt closer, then said, "Hold your gun on her, Deputy. Watch her close while I get down an' put the 'cuffs on her. An' if it happens that you got t' shoot, boy, try an' shoot her instead o' me, will you, please."

Burt gigged his roan forward until he was beside the

wagon and sitting only a few feet away from Naomi. He pointed his sawed-off shotgun practically in her face. Burt was frowning. It was obvious he did not like what he was doing. Longarm guessed he was thinking about those blow jobs and about the fact that Naomi Foster was a fine-looking piece of woman flesh. A load of sixteen-gauge number-two goose shot would shred that flesh badly.

"Just do your duty, Burt," Longarm said as he swung down off the buckskin and approached the wagon on foot, a set of steel handcuffs dangling from his hand.

"Turn around, Naomi. You've had your one chance t' slip away. There won't be another." Longarm put a foot on the front axle to step up onto the wagon.

"Fuck you, bastard!" Naomi snapped. And pulled a very familiar-looking pistol out of her skirt pocket.

Chapter 51

"Shoot, deputy!" Longarm barked.

He had the handcuffs in his right hand and his left was holding onto the side of the wagon box so he could climb up into it. Burt, on the other hand, had the shotgun pointed at Naomi.

"Shoot!"

The young deputy sat as if frozen, his finger on the trigger but not moving.

Naomi was certainly willing to move.

She pointed the Smith & Wesson .44 down at Longarm and pulled the trigger. The gun spat fire and lead, and Longarm felt a burning in his right thigh.

The impact of the bullet jerked his leg to the side.

Longarm threw the handcuffs at Naomi in an attempt to spoil her aim. He clawed at the .45 in its holster and fired.

His first shot, fired at virtually point-blank range, struck the woman in the belly and doubled her up.

His second hit her high in the chest.

And a third, more carefully aimed, hit her on the bridge of her nose.

Naomi's head snapped back and she dropped to the floor of the wagon box like a marionette with its strings slashed.

Longarm gritted his teeth against the burning in his leg. He carefully punched the spent cartridge casings out of his Colt and reloaded before doing anything else. Then he dropped his britches to take a look at the wound.

It was a surface wound, elongated and painful but not serious. It likely would leave a scar, something to join his collection of them. He pulled a handkerchief from his pocket and used it to dab at the wound.

"I have some bandages and stuff for emergencies," the wagon master said, coming up behind Longarm.

"That'd help. Thanks."

Burt Hood continued to sit on his roan. He had his sawed-off in hand but had lowered it. Now he dropped the weapon, allowing it to dangle on its leather keeper.

"Can I . . . can I help?" he asked softly.

"You could've a minute ago," Longarm snarled, wincing at the pain as he moved his leg. The movement started the blood flowing again.

The wagon master, George, returned with a roll of clean bandage material. He knelt and carefully wound a wrap around and around Longarm's thigh until he was satisfied, then ripped the cloth and tied it off.

"That's better, friend. Thank you," Longarm said.

"I'm sorry it had to be done," George said. "Look, I . . . we didn't know she was wanted for anything. We just took her at her word that she needed to get north and couldn't wait for the stagecoach. That's besides being broke. She was hungry and a mite bedraggled, and we took her in."

"You did the right thing," Longarm said. "You were just trying to help. There's no harm in that."

Thomas, standing in the driving box of his wagon, grinned and said, "She sure gave great blow jobs though."

"Damnit, Thomas, we weren't going to say anything about that," George snapped.

"Sorry. I forgot."

George looked at Longarm, his expression sheepish, the kid caught with his hand in the cookie jar. "She did, though."

Longarm laughed. "That was the way she paid for her passage? Well, there wasn't any harm in it."

"Say, deputy, what should we do with, um, with the body?" George asked.

"I really don't much care, friend. Toss her out alongside the road if you like or carry her on to Thermopolis an' let the folks there start themselves a cemetery. Whatever you like."

"I expect we'll want to see she gets a Christian burial anyhow. You say her name wasn't Susan?"

"It was Naomi Foster." Longarm spelled the name to make sure the teamster got it right for the headstone if there was one.

Longarm caught up the reins of the buckskin and mounted. Burt had not said a word nor done a thing in some time. He continued to sit atop the rented roan horse.

Longarm looked at him and said, "Let's go, kid. We got a long ride back to Rawlins."

"Yes, sir," Burt said, his voice and expression meek and small.

Longarm led out with the buckskin. Burt followed well behind on the roan.

Chapter 52

They left the Union Pacific eastbound at Cheyenne.

"I need to find the Western Union office," Burt said. "There should be some money waiting there for me. I wired my uncle from Rawlins. He should have some cash waiting there and I can repay you for taking care of me since I got robbed."

"That ain't necessary," Longarm said. He had barely spoken to Burt ever since the young man froze instead of shooting Naomi Foster.

"I feel like it is, Longarm. I owe you. More than just money, too. I owe you for a lot of things."

Longarm grunted but did not reply.

He followed Burt to the Western Union office where he got a voucher, then to the First Citizens Bank of Cheyenne where five hundred dollars was waiting in the name of C. Burton Hood.

"How much do you figure I owe you?" Burt asked. "The cash, I mean. There is no way I could ever repay the other lessons you gave me."

Longarm shrugged. "Call it even, kid. I don't want any-thing from you."

"At least take this," he said, handing Longarm a pair of gold double eagles.

Longarm grunted again and dropped the coins into his pocket. It was too much, but he was not going to stand there and argue with the young man.

"There is something else," Burt said. "Something . . . I don't know exactly how to say this, but law enforcement just is not for me. I admire you and what you do, but I could never . . ."

"You could never bring yourself t' shoot a woman, even if she was tryin' to shoot you. Or your partner," Longarm said. "Yeah, I kinda figured that, kid."

"Back there on the trail . . . with Naomi . . . and it didn't have anything to do with her sucking me off like she did, or fucking me, which I have to admit she also did . . . it didn't have anything to do with that, Longarm. She was a woman, and I just couldn't shoot her. Shooting geese and deer and the like, that just isn't the same thing as shooting another human being, man or woman either one. I . . . I'm just not cut out for this, Longarm. I hope you understand."

"It's better for us both t' know it, kid, than for you t' someday get yourself or some other deputy killed." He removed his Stetson and ran a hand through his hair. "I'll tell Billy Vail when I get back to the office, kid. You go on home to Maryland an' drink your Jespers rye an' screw your lady friends an' forget about this whole experience. You're a nice boy, Burt, but you ain't no deputy United States marshal."

"Yes, sir. I'm sorry it didn't work out." Burt turned away. So did Longarm. He had told Burt the truth, though. It was better that they all know sooner than later or Burt's inability to pull the trigger could get someone killed, damn near had gotten Longarm killed.

And that would have really pissed him off, Longarm thought with a wry smile.

The smile expanded into joyful anticipation as he headed toward Amanda Reese's home.

Chapter 53

Amanda's sheets were scented. Lilac, he thought. Or, hell, it could be something else. He was not into scented sheets himself but did not mind them. In fact, cool and flowery, they were pleasant.

So was Amanda. She took her time at her makeup table brushing her hair. And using the contents of a perfume bottle, too, he noticed. Her face powder smelled good enough without the perfume, but he was not complaining. The woman was handsome and tasty.

Sitting on that makeup stool, which appeared much too flimsy for Amanda's mature figure, she could have been posing for a painting. A painting of a nude, a cherub perhaps or a wood nymph. The better hotels down in Denver had such paintings in their gentlemen's bars.

He propped up on one elbow and admired her while she gave herself the requisite number of brush strokes.

"How many strokes tonight, 'Manda?"

"One hundred, dear. *Every* night. Do you mind waiting while I finish?"

"Hell, darlin', you look so pretty doin' it that I'd be a mighty low sort to complain about it." He stretched and wiggled his toes. But he did not close his eyes. Not with all that beauty on display.

Finally Amanda reached a hundred and laid the hairbrush aside. She dabbed a little more perfume on, this time beneath her arms and underneath her tits, too. Then she turned, stood, came to him.

Longarm was more than ready for her. His cock was standing tall, throbbing slightly in anticipation.

Amanda climbed onto him without preamble, straddling his waist and guiding Longarm's cock into her pussy. She was already wet, giving herself away that she had been anticipating this every bit as much as he had.

She moaned as Longarm filled her, and he began to raise his hips to her, sliding up and down, in and out, while Amanda pumped her hips.

She reached behind her and toyed with his balls while they fucked, driving Longarm half out of his mind with pure sensation.

After little more than a minute Amanda cried out. Her pussy lips clenched tight around him as she reached a climax ahead of him.

"You ready for some more, darlin'?" he teased.

"I'm ready for everything you can give me."

"Good," Longarm responded. He reached up, threw her down onto her scented sheets, and began driving into Amanda's body as hard and as rapidly as he could. He did not stop until he hosed the inside of her cunt with all the jism he had stored up in his balls.

Only then, with a contented sigh, did he allow himself to relax on top of Amanda's generous body and pillow his head on her tits.

Chapter 54

He spent the night—a quite delightful night it was, too—
with Amanda, woke to the feel of his dick in her mouth, and
came there, gently, as the perfect start to a new day.

When she had sucked the last droplets of come from his
cock, he stroked the back of her head and sighed, then sat up.

"Can you stay the day, Custis?" she asked, sitting up and
wiping her lips with the back of her hand. "It would be fun."

Longarm shook his head. "Sorry, darlin'. I have t' get
back down to Denver an' file my report about all that's gone
wrong this time out."

Amanda pouted, "You don't have to tell your boss everything, Custis. You could stay one more day. He would never
even know."

"Oh, but I'd know," Longarm said. He sat up on the side
of the comfortable four-poster and began dressing.

"Then let me at least fix breakfast for you," Amanda said.
"You will stay for breakfast, won't you?"

"That I will be glad t' do," he said. "I'll want to eat someplace, an' I'd rather it be with you than with strangers." He

leaned forward and kissed her on the forehead. "Go on now. Get the fire going while I finish here," he said, buckling his gun belt around his hips.

An hour later, his belly warm with a fine meal, he kissed Amanda at the doorway, then tipped his hat to the lady. "You're a fine lass, Mrs. Reese." He winked. "An' a splendid fuck as well."

"Good-bye, Custis. Do come again." She laughed, making sure he understood the full meaning of what she was saying. She also reached down and gave his dick a furtive squeeze, careful to make sure the neighbors could not see.

Longarm walked to the railroad depot and approached the ticket window.

Behind him he heard a gasp from someone on the platform, then the dull, flat report of a gunshot.

A bullet thumped into the framing that surrounded the ticket window.

Longarm spun, .45 in hand, to see a man wearing a gray suit and narrow-brim hat, to all outward appearances a gentleman traveling on business, taking aim for a second shot.

The man had a dark complexion and a full mustache.

And he had only seconds to live.

Chapter 55

Longarm reloaded his .45, then walked across the railroad platform and knelt beside the body of the businessman who had just tried to kill him. A Cheyenne police officer was quickly on the scene.

"What happened here?" the young policeman demanded.

Longarm explained and said, "Damn if I know what's going on. People keep tryin' to kill me, and I don't know why."

He picked up the dead assassin's pistol and shook his head. It had been worn in a shoulder holster. Longarm pushed the dead man's coat back and returned the pistol to the leather.

"You don't know this man?" the policeman asked.

"No, I surely don't. Let's see if he has anything on him that would identify 'im." Longarm searched the man's pockets. He found a pipe and tobacco pouch, a clean handkerchief, a pair of spectacles in a leather case, and fourteen silver pesos.

Inside the spectacles case he also found a carefully folded wanted poster. Or what looked like a wanted poster anyway. It was written in Spanish.

The only things Longarm could make out on it were the words "Custis Long" and the figures "P3,000."

Three thousand pesos on his head? It made no sense.

"Can you read this?" he asked the Cheyenne policeman.

"I have a little Spanish. Let me see it."

Longarm handed the sheet up to the cop, who scratched the side of his nose while he read. Then the man said, "There are some words here that I don't know, but the gist of it is that whoever broadcast this flyer wants the head . . . that's what it says, I'm pretty sure . . . wants the actual head of whoever this Custis Long person is. Wants it delivered to a man name of Juan Ariel Valdes."

"Never heard of him," Longarm said. "Does it say where this head is to be delivered?"

"Some address in Denver," the cop said. "At least I think that's what it is saying." He handed the printed sheet back to Longarm and said, "I'm glad I'm not this Custis Long fellow. Three thousand is a hell of a lot of money. It's enough to have every gunman north of the border on the prod for him."

"Do you need any formal statement from me?" Longarm asked.

"No, I don't think so. There were plenty of witnesses who say you shot in self-defense," the policeman said.

"Then if you will excuse me, I want to catch the next train south," Longarm told the young man. He stood, his knee joints cracking, and returned to the ticket window and the battered carpetbag he had dropped there when the shooting started.

Chapter 56

Denver was crowded and noisy and smoky and . . . home. Longarm was glad to get back. Before he even stopped at his boardinghouse or at the nearby Chinese laundry, he climbed into a cab and told the driver to take him to the Federal Building.

"Long!" Billy Vail's clerk Henry cried when he saw Longarm enter the U.S. marshals' offices. "Where have you been? The boss has been trying to find you for days."

Longarm blinked. That was not his usual reception here. "What's wrong, Henry?"

"I should let him tell you, but . . . the rumor is that someone has put a price on your head, Custis. Your actual head, I mean. Someone wants to have your head brought to him in a basket. Except you aren't John the Baptist, and you're still using your head. At least I hope you are."

"I only found out about it myself late yesterday afternoon," Longarm said. "Three thousand pesos is the payment if somebody kills me. That's the same as three thousand dollars. Shit, man, that's more than five years' wages."

"Wait here, Custis. Let me tell the boss that you're here. And you are alive. Safe and alive." Henry smiled. "He will be as glad to get that news as I am."

The mousy little clerk, who could be a tiger when called upon, leaped out from behind his desk and ran into Billy Vail's private office without even bothering to knock. He was back out within seconds, holding the door open and motioning for Longarm to enter.

"Come in, Longarm. Has Henry told you about the price on your head?" Vail said.

"Boss, you actually seem happy t' see me for a change," Longarm said, laughing.

"This is no laughing matter, Longarm. This is serious business. The sort that could get you killed," Billy Vail said. The boss got up from behind his desk and came around to grab Longarm by the shoulders and give him a shake, as close as Billy Vail ever came to hugging his deputy. "Are you all right?" he asked.

"I'm fine, Boss. An' I know what son of a bitch has put that reward out on me."

Longarm pulled the wanted poster from his pocket and unfolded it before handing it to Vail. "I don't read Spanish, but a fella up in Cheyenne told me pretty much what it says."

"Son of a bitch!" Billy snarled. "Putting a price on one of my deputies . . ." He quickly read the flyer, then shook his head. "Valdes. The name doesn't ring any bells. How do you know the man. Longarm?"

"That's what puzzles me, Boss. I don't know him from Adam's off ox. Never heard of him before this. Still don't know who the hell he is." Longarm's expression became a grim smile. "But I am for damn sure fixin' to find out."

Billy grunted softly, still looking at the flyer. "I can get a squad of deputies here tomorrow morning, and we can go pay a call on the gentleman," he said.

"If you don't mind, Boss," Longarm replied, "I'd just as soon handle this m'self. It's personal with me, not official."

"I am making it official," Billy Vail said. "This is an assault on an employee of the United States government. That makes it official. That makes it the business of this office."

"Whatever you say, Boss, but I want t' handle it," Longarm said.

"All right. It is an assignment. Bring this Valdes in, Custis. Under arrest. While you are doing that, I will get with the United States attorney to see what charges can be brought against the man. Fair enough?"

"On my way, Boss." Longarm spun on his heels and headed out again.

Chapter 57

He left his carpetbag full of dirty laundry on the floor behind Henry's desk, but he did open it and grab a handful of extra .45 cartridges that he dropped loose in his coat pocket.

"Looking to start a war, Custis?" Henry asked.

"I damn sure might do that," Longarm responded. "Oh, I almost forgot. I need a warrant. I don't want anyone t' ever doubt that this was done legal. Can you get a judge t' sign off on one real quick, hoss?"

"You know that I can," Henry said. "What name do you want on it?"

"Juan Ariel Valdes," Longarm said.

"And this Valdes fellow would be . . . ?"

"He's the son of a bitch that put the price on my head. Says it right on the flyer that says he wants my head." Longarm grinned. "He wants my head? Well, I'm gonna take it to him. But still attached t' my shoulders, thank you very much."

"Wait here, Longarm. I'll get your warrant. What charge

do you want on it? Assault on a federal peace officer? How does that sound. It should only be a few minutes."

Henry was as good as his word. He was gone from the office not more than twenty minutes before he returned with a warrant for the arrest of Valdes on a charge of assault on a federal officer.

"Do you want me to back you up?" Henry offered.

Longarm gripped Henry's shoulder and gave him a friendly shake. "Thanks, old friend, but this is something I want t' do on my own. It's . . . I suppose you would say it's a matter o' pride."

"Whatever you think, Longarm, but be careful. There is something very wrong about the sort of person who would make such a public reward offer. Whoever this man is, he must be powerful."

"Nobody is this powerful," Longarm said, holding up the wanted poster with his name on it. "Not only is he fucking with the law, he's fucking with me. Personal. So by all means, let's go ahead an' make this just as personal as it gets. I'll bring the son of a bitch in in handcuffs. Or dead. An' I don't much care which."

Longarm spun around and headed out of the U.S. marshals' office and onto the streets of Denver.

He hailed a cab and before he entered it pulled out the wanted flyer again to give the driver the street address of Juan Ariel Valdes.

Son of a bitch wanted his head? Well, he was going to get it.

Chapter 58

The address meant nothing to Longarm. He sat inside the hansom and watched the city unfold outside the window as the cab traveled to the southwestern edge of town. It stopped outside a large, turreted house with a lawn large enough to graze a few head of goats on.

"Do you want me to wait?" the cabbie offered. "If you'll be going back to the city soon, you won't find another cab anywhere nearby, mister."

"Yeah. Good idea." Longarm smiled grimly. "I doubt my business here will take very long."

The cabbie set his brake and wrapped the driving lines around his whip socket, then tipped his hat down over his eyes and appeared to fall asleep on the box. His horse dropped its head and it, too, seemed to sleep.

Longarm let himself in through a gate in the white picket fence that surrounded the four-story gray house.

When he mounted the steps to the front porch a large man wearing white gloves and a swallowtail coat stepped out in front of him. Despite his fancy trappings the man's many times flattened nose and a cauliflower ear gave away his true profession.

"Are you Valdes?" Longarm asked, knowing the answer before he uttered the question.

"You have a appointment, bub?" the bodyguard asked although he, too, surely knew the answer to his question before he went through the formality of asking it.

"No appointment, but I do have the head of Custis Long," Longarm truthfully said.

"You serious, man?" the bodyguard gaped. "You have it?"

"I do," Longarm said.

"Where is it? I want to see."

"In due time," Longarm said. "Now do I see Valdes or not?"

"Let me go tell him. Wait here. No, forget that. Come inside." The big fellow held the door for Longarm to enter.

Past the vestibule Longarm entered a foyer that was larger than some houses he had known.

"The parlor is over there. Have a seat. I'll tell the man you're here," the guard said.

Longarm followed the direction to a richly furnished parlor with a fireplace big enough for roasting oxen. It held nothing but cold ashes at the moment, but he stood beside it anyway and leaned an elbow on the marble mantelpiece.

Somewhere upstairs he heard a shouting match between a man and a woman, the screaming conducted in Spanish, followed by the sound of footsteps coming down the curved staircase that led up from the foyer to the second floor and beyond.

Longarm's grim smile returned as he was joined by a pudgy man, short and plump and balding, gray where he still had hair. He was wearing a smoking jacket and a puffy, silk cravat. He looked delighted at the prospect of receiving the head of Custis Long.

Not so pleased was the woman who trailed along behind him. She was red faced with fury.

Until she saw Longarm.

He bowed toward her and said, "Afternoon, Maria Lourdes. How're you today?"

Maria Lourdes—he had completely forgotten that her last name was Valdes—gaped as if unable to speak.

"You, sir," Maria Lourdes' husband said. "You have news about this Custis Long? You've brought me his head? I have the money for you. Will have as soon as you produce the head." Valdes's English was perfect; he barely had an accent.

When Longarm had been fucking Maria Lourdes she said that while she came to Denver to shop, her husband came on business. Longarm had not minded cuckolding the man as long as Maria Lourdes did not seem to care.

Now it appeared that the husband did care. At least three thousand dollars' worth.

The anger that had been simmering inside Longarm suddenly evaporated. The truth was that he could not blame the man for being pissed off. A stranger *had* been fucking the man's wife, after all. And she *was* a wife, duly wedded.

It was obvious that Valdes cared deeply for the woman despite her straying ways. He forgave her and placed his anger on the unknown stranger, who in this case just happened to be Custis Long.

If he had known . . .

"I have the head of Custis Long," Longarm quite truthfully said, "but I don't want your money. I just . . . wanted you t' know. So you can call off the hunt now. It's over. Done with."

Longarm looked at Maria Lourdes and frowned. He suddenly had the feeling that the plump little man in front of him deserved better than a cheating wife.

He thought about the arrest warrant in his coat pocket, thought that the paper could stay right where it was.

Longarm forced back an impulse to apologize to the little man. "I, uh, I just wanted you t' know. So call off your dogs. It's over."

"You will not accept the reward?" Valdes asked.

Longarm shook his head. "No, sir. No reward."

"I would be glad to pay," Valdes said.

"No, what I done had nothing t' do with money," Longarm said.

"Ah. Honor. This I understand, senor."

Honor. The word stung Longarm. He looked again at Maria Lourdes. The faithless bitch seemed amused by this exchange between her cuckolded husband and the man who had done the dirty.

Juan Ariel Valdes deserved better, Longarm thought. Which he probably knew, but he loved the woman anyway.

Longarm looked at the big bodyguard who was lurking in the doorway. Just doing his job with nothing personal, just professional.

Not that there was any danger here.

"I just wanted you t' know, sir," Longarm said. "Now if you will excuse me, I have a cab waiting outside."

Longarm touched the brim of his Stetson toward the sad little man and followed the bodyguard to the front door, ignoring Maria Lourdes as he brushed past her.

He did fleetingly wonder how many of those flyers had been distributed. And how many more men might be wanting to collect that bounty.

Bitch! he thought.

Watch for

LONGARM AND THE DEADLY SISTERS

the 430th novel in the exciting LONGARM
series from Jove

Coming in September!

LONGARM

GIANT-SIZED ADVENTURE FROM AVENGING ANGEL LONGARM.

BY TABOR EVANS

penguin.com/actionwesterns